Hodge-Podge: Short Stories and Poems

By Brunislaw (Benji) Wozniak

Dedicated to Ann Wozniak,

Patricia Clark, Kimberly Wozniak

TABLE OF CONTENTS

"I Consider Myself A Pen
And The World My Paper"

— Brunislaw (Benji) Wozniak

A COMMON CHRISTMAS

Steve started as Teme lay before him, moving her arms and legs up and down. They had only been going out for three months, but she mesmerized him. He honestly had no plans on asking her to be his girlfriend. When he first met her, it was her best friend Grace, a blonde-haired, blue eyed girl who in all rights was supposed to be the girl he hooked up with. The black haired Filipino girl hadn't even been a second thought to him. If Grace didn't have detention that day, it probably would have ended up that way. However, she did and when he and Teme went back to his house to wait, one thing led to another, and a tickle fight turned into a kissing match. She wasn't what he wanted. She wasn't what he had been looking for, but now she seemed to be all he ever needed.

"You're going to catch your death of a cold," he said, smiling down at her. "Not to mention you look ridiculous."

"I'm making a snow angel," she said as she stood up and shook the snow off her back. "So how'd I do?"

Steve looked at the place where the impression of the snow angel was and started laughing.

"What's so funny?" Teme asked, looking at him confused. "Didn't it turn out alright?"

"Sure," Steve smiled. "I just didn't know angels had horns and a pointed tail."

"Oh! You're such a jerk!" Teme said as she hit him playfully on the chest with her snow covered mittens. The mist coming off her mittens made him laugh even harder. He spun her to him and held her close as they both looked down at her creation.

"I'm glad we came. I've never been to the Boston Commons during Christmas time. It's really beautiful," she said, leaning her back against him.

"Yeah, it's cool how they strung up all the Christmas lights and hung all the different decorations around the common light poles.I wasn't sure I was going to like it, but I'm glad we came too," he replied as he took her hand, and they started walking.

During Christmas a large tree is decorated in front of the Boston State House. One of the time-honored traditions is the lighting of the Christmas tree. The whole city comes alive for the event, and you can watch ice sculptures being formed or listen to carolers sing on the steps of the State House. A portion of the Commons is watered, frozen, and smoothed to create an ice skating area.

"I've been thinking," Teme said as they walked. "Did you know that all great relationships have a song?"

"We've only been going out for three months," Steve replied. "I mean. I don't really think that we've reached great status as far as relationships go."

"So you don't think we have a great relationship?" Teme said, stopping and staring at Steve with a pouty face and making her lower lip puff in and out as she spoke.

"I didn't say that," Steve said.

"I knew you'd agree," Teme said, grabbing his arm and moving him along before he could finish saying anything else. "So we need to decide on a song. I like Journey's Faithfully. What do you think?"

"Honestly, I have no idea. This is all new to me. How about that love song by Guns N' Roses. It sounds decent." Steve replied confused.

"You do know he's singing about his dog and how he had to put it down right?" Teme said with a puzzled look on her face. "Do I look like a dog to you?"

"Well, you do have a nice tail," Steve said with a smile.

"That's it!" Teme said, throwing her hands in the air. "It's official, you're a pig!"

"Hey, I was only kidding," Steve said, trying to hold back a laugh. "Look Faithfully by Journey is fine. I like it."

"I knew you would, I mean, it's perfect, it's about a love that's eternal. It fits us to a tee, it's so adorable," Teme said with a big grin on her face.

"Adora.... What?" Steve asked as he stopped walking and looked at her questioningly.

"Adorabibble," Teme replied. "It means beyond adorable."

"I'm failing English, but I'm sure that's not a real word!" Steve said, shaking his head.

"It's my word and that's all that matters," Teme replied. "Oh look, Santa hats."

Steve had to excuse himself and Teme as she dragged him through the crowd of sightseers to a vendor's stand. The man behind the counter was heavy set and balding. Steve could tell he'd been attending the stand for a while because his cheeks were bright red.

"Am I reading that sign right?" Steve asked. 'Does that say twelve dollars for a Santa's hat?'

"Yes, and for another two dollars, I can put the lovely young lady's name on it with glitter," the vendor replied.

"Fourteen dollars," Steve said in shock. "That's a case of beer and a few munchies."

"What?" Teme asked, looking at him with a lost look on her face. "What are you talking about?"

"Man-math," Steve and the vendor both said at the same time.

"Excuse me?" Teme said as she stared at both of them, waiting for them to explain.

"Man-math," Steve replied with a smile. "It's when a girl wants a man to buy her something and we think of what else we could buy with the money."

"But don't you think I'd look cute in one of these?" Teme said, taking one of the hats off the counter and placing it on her head.

"Trickanometry," the vendor said with a laugh.

"Now, what's that?" Teme asked, placing both hands on her hips and scrunching her face up in a fake expression of anger.

"Trickanometry is when a girl resorts to trying to trick a man into buying her something, by saying how sexy or cute they'd look in the object they want," Steve replied.

"Fine, I don"t want the stupid hat anyway," Teme said placing the hat back on the counter. "I just thought you'd like how it looked on me, that's all."

"Oh she's good!" The vendor chuckled. "She's a keeper,son."

"One hat with her name on it, please," Steve said as he reached into his sock to pull out his money.

"Why do you have a wallet in your back pocket, but keep your money in your sock?" Teme asked.

"It's so if anyone swipes my wallet, all they'll get is an empty wallet and not my money," Steve said as he paid the vendor and explained to him how to spell Teme's name so it could be placed on the hat with glitter.

"Thank you," Teme said to the vendor as she placed the finished hat on her head and playfully skipped down the path. She stopped and looked back over her shoulder with an impish grin. "Are you coming with me or not?'

"You are in for it with that one my friend," the vendor said with a laugh. "But, I'll say this again, she's definitely a keeper."

"Yeah, you're right about that! Have a Merry Christmas," Steve said as he raced to catch up with Teme.

When he caught up with her, she was standing on the edge of the ice skating area. She was leaning against a tree watching the people sail across the ice. Some looked graceful' it seemed as if they were born with skates on their feet and others looked as if they were beyond terrified to be on the ice.

"Do you know how to skate?" Teme asked as she turned to him and he moved closer to her.

"In my case, it's more of an ice walk than actually skating," Steve laughed. "I've never been good at ice skating. Now roller skating, I must admit, I'm really good at that."

"Then you'll have to take me roller skating sometime." Teme said as she grabbed his hand and led him down the path.

"Absolutely, I can't think of anyone I'd rather couple skate with," Steve said with a smile as he took her arm in his and walked. "Bedsides, now we can request our song while we skate."

"I've been thinking," Teme said, looking at him with that impish smile of hers.

"Oh, God, I'm in trouble!" Steve said, trying to hold back a laugh.

"You're not funny," Teme replied with a pouty expression on her face.

"Who's joking?" Steve smiled. "Whenever you say, 'you've been thinking,' I'm usually in for it."

"It's just that now that we have a song, we should have special names for each other," Teme said with a smile.

"Are you suggesting that we call each other sappy names like, Snuggle Bunny or something like that? Steve asked, stopping and looking at teme as if she'd lost her mind.

"Don't look at me like that, in every great relationship, they had pet names for each other," Teme said to him as if this was common knowledge everyone should know.

"Was I supposed to get an instruction manual or something when I

13

asked you out?" Steve said with a smile. "Because I've never heard any of this stuff before."

"I didn't expect you to know this stuff, you're a guy," Teme said. "But now that you have me, I can steer you right."

"I heard about your type," Steve laughed

"What type is that?" Teme asked, looking at him confused.

"You're going to suggest that I change my hairstyle. Then, maybe how I dress or the music I listen to, and then, once I do all that you'll turn around and dump me because I'm no longer the guy you fell in love with!" Steve said with a laugh.

"You're a jerk," Teme said as she crossed her arms and turned her back on him.

"Hey, I'm only joking," Steve said, gently placing his hand on her shoulder. "I'd love to hear what your ideas for pet names are."

"I knew you would," Teme said, spinning around towards him with a big grin. "Okay, with your brown hair and hazel eyes, I decided Pookey would be a great name for you."

"Poo...what?" Steve asked with a confused look on his face. "What kind of name is that?"

"Pookey, he"s Garfield the cat's teddy bear, Teme smiled. "He's so soft and cuddly! Don't you want to be my Pookey Bear?"

"Hell No!" Steve said, shaking his head. "That's way too wimpy. You need to think of another name."

"Okay, fine," Teme said with a devious grin on her face. "I'll just tell all your friends and mine how adorabibble you are."

"You wouldn't," Steve said with a shocked look on his face.

"We'll see," Teme said with a smile.

"So, how do you spell that? With an 'ie' or a 'y'?" Steve asked in a defeated tone,

"That would be with an 'ey'," Teme said, taking his arm in hers and

14

continuing down the path. "So what name do you think fits me best?"

"Evil," Steve laughed.

"I'm going to ignore that," Teme said with a smile. "I know it's just the cold weather warping your train of thought."

"Touche," Steve replied jokingly. "I was thinking of something along the lines of Cuddles."

"I like it." Teme said happily. "Pookey loves Cuddles. It has sort of a rhyme to it."

"These pet names are just between us, right? I mean, you're not going to call me that name around everyone, are you?" Steve said, looking at her concerned.

"Oh calm down. I wouldn't embarrass you like that. Those names are strictly between us." Teme laughed. "But a little black'mail never hurt."

"I'm still leaning towards Evil," Steve said as he pulled her close to him.

As they got to the Boston State House they could see its golden dome. They could hear the crowd counting down to the lighting of the Christmas tree. Steve didn't know who started the countdown or even if the number they were yelling was correct. However, when the crowd reached zero the whole tree burst into a dazzle of different colored lights.The large star on the top was a bright gold and the whole crowd let out a collective awe at the sight of it.

"Have you ever seen anything so beautiful that it just takes your breath away?" Teme asked, leaning into him.

"Yeah, I actually have." Steve said softly, but his eyes weren't looking at the tree.

THE COLD HARD TRUTH

Steve crouched behind the old station wagon and stared at the street light. The light had turned red and a car was stopped waiting for it to change. Steve raced out once the light turned green and grabbed onto the car rear bumper. As he was sliding down the ice covered street with the car he looked back and saw that Teme hadn't budged from where they had been standing. So he released his grip on the bumper and slid to the sidewalk.

"What gives," he asked as he raced back to where she was standing. "You were supposed to do exactly as I did."

"Are you insane?" Teme shouted, staring at him angrily. "You could have been killed!"

"I...." he started to speak, but was cut off.

"I, nothing! If you fell on that ice a car behind would have run over and killed you. Do you think I came out in this cold to watch my boy-friend get squished like a bug? Is that what you were thinking when you asked me to come out with you? Well, was it?" she demanded with her arms now folded and a now serious upgrade from angry to furious look on her face.

Steve really wanted to laugh, but knew better. It was just that Teme looked so cute. She was all bundled up to protect herself from the cold. Her long black hair was sticking out of a black stocking cap with a fuzzy ball on top. Her cheeks and nose were already red in the short time it had taken them to walk from his house to where they were now standing on Franklin St.

"I'm sorry! I really didn't mean to scare you, honestly," he said, as he sighed and walked over and gave her a hug.

"Well you did, ya big jerk! That's what you and your friends do for fun? You see who can commit suicide the fastest!," she said, pulling out of his grip and looking at him questioningly.

"It's called car skiing, and we do it every winter. The only danger is if you hit a manhole cover and wipe. I can't even begin to tell you how often I bruised a hip or elbow from hitting the street. Then there's cab drivers. You don't want to grab onto a cabs bumper. Because if they see you they will literally stop the cab and chase you away," he explained.

"I'm in love with a lunatic," Teme sighed, raising a mitted hand to her head as if she had a sudden headache and walked past Steve.

"Hey, com on Tem," Steve said, as he jogged to catch up to her. "You're the one who wanted to know what me and my friends do for fun."

"You don't see the danger in what you're doing?" Teme asked as they walked.

"Well, yeah! I guess, but that's kind of what makes it fun. It's the danger I guess and not to mention it's a challenge. You have to sneak up on the car without being seen. Then grab onto and hold the bumper as the car speeds up and you're sliding down the street. I think you'd like it if you gave it a try," he said, as they made their way down Franklin Street towards Central Square.

"No. I'll pass, but are there any other things like this that you and your friends do that I should know about." she asked.

"Well, we do go up to the train tracks and snow jump," he replied, hoping she wouldn't ask for him to give details on what was.

"That doesn't sound so bad. What exactly do you guys do," she asked with a big smile.

"Damn it!" Steve thought to himself. He should've never even mentioned it. He could always lie about what it was, but that wouldn't be right. He was always told relationships were built on trust and he really

17

didn't want to break the trust he and Teme had.

"Well, we go up to the railroad tracks and wait for a train to come by and slow down. Then we run up and grab onto the handles and as the trail speeds up we jump off into snowbanks," he said, with a sigh, anticipating her response.

"Did I call you a Lunatic?" Teme asked, shaking her head.

"Yeah, you covered that already." Steve laughed.

"Good, I would' want you to think that I thought these were intelligent decisions." She said angrily.

"Hey, come on! You haven't done anything like what me and my friends do," he asked.

"I've gone to the reservoir and jumped off the pump house during the summer," she replied with a smile.

"Ya see, that's dangerous." Steve replied as he reached down and held her hand as they walked.

"Only if you jump on the side where the water intake is. But no one's dumb enough to do that." Teme said, as she leaned in closer to him. "So, have any of your friends gotten hurt snow jumping?"

"Not on the train tracks, but my friend Kenny got hurt doing something like it." Steve said, immediately regretting it once it left his mouth. There was no way this conversation was going to end well on his part.

"So, tell me what happened." Teme said, with a look that said you are about to prove my point for me.

"Okay, a bunch of us climbed a building that the plows had pushed a pile of snow against. So, there were a bunch of snow banks for us to jump into. The thing is when Kenny jumped he landed on a snow covered dumpster.

Once he finished his story he knew he would never be able to justify to Teme things he and his friends did were fun and not dangerous.

"Oh my God! How bad was he hurt?" Teme asked with a concerned look on her face.

"He broke both his legs and fractured his pelvis. He had to wear a cast on the lower half of his body for almost a year." Steve sighed.

"See, see that's what I'm talking about. That could have been you." Teme said, shaking her head.

"Tem, listen, you're right, but it wasn't! I'm not going to say that the stuff we do isn't risky, because it is. The thing is, it's a lot of fun, so we take the risk," he said.

"Are we going someplace now that falls into that crazy category you call fun," she asked.

"We're going to Goldfish Pond, to bucky jump." Steve smiled. "You're going to have a blast."

"We're going where, to do what?" Teme asked, looking at him with a puzzled expression.

"To Goldfish Pond. It's a circular pond, with a circular island in the middle. During the summer they put flowers on the island in the shape of a goldfish and actually fill the pond with actual goldfish. During the winter when the pond freezes over, we break the ice into large pieces and try to run or jump across the pieces to the island and back again." He laughed. "Bucky Jumping!"

"What if you fall into the water? You'd catch your death from the cold." Teme said concerned.

"Then I better not fall in." Steve said with a big smile. "Then again, you could come over and spoon feed me chicken soup when I'm sick. I think I'd like that!"

"Dream on Romeo," she giggled. "I see your future and nowhere in it does it have me spoon feeding you chicken soup!"

"Come on, I want to take you to see something," he said, as they crossed the street at Lynn City Hall and headed towards a yellow build-ing with large picture windows.

19

"Oh!" Teme said, as she leaned closer to the window to get a better look at the display cases inside. "You brought me over here to look at engagement rings. Oh my god Steve this is so sudden!"

"What? No! I," Steve fumbled. "What I wanted to show you is around the corner. It's a bakery."

"Calm down! I was only teasing." Teme said, as she walked past him, heading in the direction he indicated the bakery was at. When she turned the corner Teme was now staring in the window of the bakery. "Are you sure you're not trying to give me some sort of hint?"

"What are you talking about?" Steve asked, looking beyond confused.

"These are wedding cakes." Teme smiled. "I think you're trying to tell me something."

"What? No! I..." Steve fumbled for words to say again.

"You are so adorable when you blush." Teme said as she opened the shop door and Steve and her stepped inside.

"Steve," a gray haired, heavyset man wearing a flour covered apron cried out! "Who is this pretty thing with you and where's Tyree?"

Tyree was Steve's friend from High School. A stocky black teen who collected comic books like Steve did. During the week they would walk to a comic book shop on Union Street located in the downtown area and on their way they would stop in and stock up on various pastries to eat from the bakery.

"Hi Mr. Apostilitis." Steve replied. "This is my girlfriend Teme. I honestly have no clue where Tyree's at, but when I see him I'll let him know you were asking about him."

"Well, what can I get you two today?" Mr. Apostilitis asked with a big smile.

"Two elephant ears and two hot cocoas would be great." Steve said, as he reached into his sock for his money.

"What are elephant ears?" Teme asked.

"Big circular pastries with cinnamon and raisins. You're going to love them." Steve said

"Sounds yummy! Oooohh macaroons! Teme said, looking into one of the cases happily.

"And four macaroons, please!" Steve added.

"Sure, sure, of course." Mr. Apostilitis said, placing his thumb and forefinger to his forehead, then going to collect the pastries.

"Did you just call me a loser?" Steve asked, in an agitated voice when Mr. Apostilitis returned.

"No, no, that's the thumb and forefinger straight up and down on the forehead. What I did was tilted sideways like a check mark for check-mate." Mr Apostilitis laughed.

"You mean like in chess?" Steve asked, looking at the bakery owner confused."

"Exactly, and that cute girl over there has you in checkmate son. Game over! You can see it written all over your face. She's captured your heart." Mr. Apostilitis said, smiling at Steve. "Don't let it get to you though, it happens to all of us."

"Check!" Teme giggled as she made the sign against her forehead and kissed Steve on the cheek.

"Now look at what you started." Steve said as he finished paying for the pastries and started to leave.

"Goodbye Mr. Apostilitis!" Teme said, as she opened the door to leave. They could hear Mr. Apostilitis saying goodbye to them as the door closed.

"He seems nice." Teme said.

"Yeah, he's a good guy." Steve said, as they ate their pastries and drank their cocoa while walking towards Central Square.

When they entered Central Square they turned onto Union Street passing all the shops and heading deeper into the downtown area.

"At night this street is supposed to be filled with drug addicts and hookers hanging around the bars." Teme said, looking around as if it was already night time and someone was going to jump out at them."

"Yeah, but most of them aren't so bad." Steve said, with a shrug of his shoulders. "They just have issues. Some are hooked on different kinds of drugs and others can"t get decent jobs, so they make money anyway they can to survive."

"That's wrongful justification! There's plenty of better and legal ways for them to make money. They just choose not to do them. Instead they make excuses as to why they continue to do the things they do, but do nothing to better their situations." Teme said, with a clear tone of disgust in her voice.

"Don't you think you're being a little harsh," Steve said. "The thing is it's not my place to judge and I don't think you should judge them either. I mean you wouldn't like it if people judged you."

"Hello, have you looked at me!" Teme said loudly.

"Of course I have." Steve replied confused at the question. "How could I not look at you, you're beautiful."

"You do realize I'm Filipino." Teme said angrily!

"So what's your point?" Steve asked.

"My point is this, all my life I've been judged and made fun of because of my looks. I've been called slant eyes, gook, chink, and numerous other insults. I could have used that as an excuse to do wrong things, but I haven"t and neither should they! There's always a better way to deal with your issues without breaking the law! That's the easy way out!"

They continued down Union Street with neither one speaking a word. Both were reflecting on what the other had said.

"I bought you a shirt." Teme finally said, breaking the silence. "I think it'll look nice on you."'

"Oh boy, I was waiting for this." Steve said, shaking his head.

"What? What are you talking about?" Teme asked.

"First you're going to suggest I change the way I dress. Then suggest my hair would look better if I had it done differently. Then suggest I might like different styles of music. Then once all these changes are made you're going to break up with me because I'll no longer be the same person you fell in love with!" Steve sighed dramatically.

"Are you joking?" Teme asked, looking at him clearly aggravated. "Because you're not funny."

"No, no, you're right it's not funny!" Because if I'm no longer the person I started as and I don't know who I've become. I'll be lost, lost!" Steve moaned and put his arm to his head in an overly dramatic gesture.

"You're a jerk!" Teme said, releasing his head and storming ahead down the street.

"Hey, I was only playing." Steve said as he ran to catch up to her and wrapped his arms around her. "You know I was only joking!"

"You know I don"t like to play games," she said as she moved to his side and took Steve's hand in hers.

"Well, I do," he said.

"Oh really," she replied with an annoyed look on her face.

"Sure, Playstation, Nintendo, Monopoly, Risk, all kinds of games!" Steve laughed.

"Those aren't the games I'm talking about," she sighed in frustration.

"I know, I know, I was only teasing," he said, with a smile. "I know you love me and I love you and I'd never play any games with you."

"Why?" Teme asked.

"Why What," he replied, confused by the question.

"Why do you love me," she asked, staring at Steve with a serious expression on her face. "And I don't want to hear, 'because you're you,' or anything like that. I want you to tell me something specific that makes you love me.'

"Fine, I'll tell you a few things," he said happily. "I love that you lay on my pill and that it smells like you after you leave. I love holding you close to me and knowing you can feel how fast my heart beats when I'm with you. I love that the other night when we fell asleep talking on the phone together and woke up in the morning you were still on the other end of the line. It made me realize that your voice is the last voice that I want to hear at night and the first voice I want to hear in the morning. That and how we both can challenge each other verbally and not be mad at one another," he sighed. "I think you bring out the best in me!"

"Oh Pookey, that was so sweet!" Teme said after a few minutes had gone by and kissed him on the cheek.

"Hey, watch that." Steve said.

"Watch What?" Teme said, looking around confused.

"The whole Pookey thing." Steve said, looking around to see if anyone he knew might be in earshot of their conversation. "Remember, that's supposed to be just between the two of us. I don't want anyone accidentally hearing that. I'd never hear the end of it.'

As they came to the end of Union Street and took a right onto Chestnut Street, Steve promised Teme that it wasn't much further. The walk was long and cold, but Steve promised that at the end it would be well worth it.

"Now it's your turn." Steve said with a smile. "Why do you love me?"

"It's a secret." Teme said with a laugh.

"What, what do you mean?" Steve asked, looking at Teme with a dumbfounded look on his face. "You seriously aren't going to tell me."

"Nope!" Teme giggled. "A girl has to have secrets."

"Hey, I just spilled my heart out to you." Steve said, agitated.

"And it was really sweet." Teme smiled. "And I promise I will tell you why I love you, just not right now, okay."

"Fine, but I was totally spot on about your nickname." Steve said.

"Cuddles!" Teme said happily."

"Nope, Evil!" Steve replied in a mockingly creepy voice.

They both laughed as they turned left at an intersection. Teme saw a small crowd gathered at what appeared to be a small man made pond. They crossed the street and stood next to a park bench. As they looked towards the pond a man jumped from one piece of floating ice onto another until he made it safely to the island in the center. Then he repeated the process until he was back onto their side of the pond again.

"Steve," a short blonde teen yelled out and jogged over to where they were standing.

"Hey Todd, what's up?" Steve said, clearly happy to see his friend.

"Just chillin', literally, brrrrr!" Todd laughed. "So who's your friend?"

"Todd, I want to introduce you to my girlfriend, Teme," Steve said happily.

"Oh, hey, what's up?" Todd said, looking at Teme curiously. "Well, come on, let's go and introduce you to the rest of the guys."

They walked over to another park bench where a small group of teen-age boys were gathered that were watching another teen jump from one piece of floating ice to another just like the man did before.

"Guys, this is Steve's new girlfriend, Teme." Todd announced as they got closer to the group.

"Hey I'm Justin," a tall skinny teen with long black hair said looking over in Teme's direction.

"What's up," a short teen with black hair said with a head nod. "I'm Peter."

"Greg," another teen with blonde hair said, holding up his hand in a mock wave.

"I'm Lance," a stocky teen with brown hair said. "And that's my brother Kenny over there crossing the ice."

"Hey!" a thin brown haired teen said, as he jumped from the floating ice to near where they were all gathered.

"Hey, it's nice to meet all of you, Steve talks about you all the time. He calls you his brothers from other mothers!" Teme said with a smile. She looked over at Kenny as it dawned on her that he was the friend Steve said was hurt badly before. Why would someone who went through such an awful ordeal be doing this crazy stuff again, she wondered.

"So are you going to give it a try?" Todd asked Teme.

"No way!" Teme said with a laugh. "I just came to watch, I'm only a spectator."

"Suit yourself." Todd said, as he walked over and jumped onto a piece of ice making his way to the island.

"I'll be right back, watch!" Steve said, with excitement in his voice as he raced over and followed Todd onto the Ice.

Teme couldn't help but notice that Steve's friends had moved away from where she was standing. She could see them talking amongst themselves and glancing over at her. She'd seen this behavior all her life. They had already decided that they wouldn't accept her. It didn't matter to them that she was Steve's girlfriend. All that mattered to them was that she wasn't white. A part of her wanted to run off and cry, but she didn't want to just leave. It would hurt Steve's feelings if she was gone when he came back. She knew how badly he wanted her to meet his friends and how disappointed he would be.

Then again, maybe he wouldn't, maybe he knew all along how they would treat her and set this whole thing up. It wouldn't be the first time someone pretended to like her only for her to end up the blount of some cruel joke. No, in her heart she just couldn't bring herself to honestly believe that. Steve was different and treated her as someone he believed was special. The only problem was that once Steve's friends told him how they felt about her he'd probably break up with her. Would he at least be kind and not do it in front of his friends and embarrass her?

Would he even have the decency to walk her back home? God she thought to herself, this is going to hurt really bad. She really was deeply in love with Steve. She heard a laugh and looked over at Steve's friends who quickly turned their heads away from her direction.

Teme watched as Steve and his friends continually crossed the ice to the island and back. She couldn't tell how much time had gone by, but she was starting to get really cold. She couldn't help but smile as Steve made his way over to her.

"So what do you think?" Steve asked happily.

"It looks like fun." Teme said through chattering teeth.

"Oh my God, Tem! Your lips are blue, you're frozen!" Steve said, concerned. "Come on, we've got to get you home and warmed up."

"No, it's okay, I'm fine, really!" Teme said, with a shiver in her voice.

"Tem, I wanted to show you what Buckey Jumping was. Well, you've seen it, you're freezing, and now we're leaving. End of story!" Steve said, firmly. "Besides, I really don't want to have to feed you chicken soup in bed."

"Tomato soup and grilled cheese." Teme said, through chattering teeth and a big smile.

"What? What are you talking about?" Steve asked.

"I don't like chicken soup. I like tomato soup with grilled cheese when I'm sick." Teme said with a laugh.

"Whatever, we're getting you home and warmed up." Steve said with a smile as he turned from her and headed back over to his friends. "Hey guys, Teme's freezing, so I'm going to take her home."

"Yeah, that's cool." Kenny replied. "Are you coming down this weekend?"

"I think so, why? What's up?" Steve asked, trying to hurry the conversation along so he could go back to Teme and take her home.

"Just you, right!" Todd asked, emphasizing the words just you!

"I think so, why?" Steve asked questioningly.

"To be honest, we don"t want you to bring Teme around anymore." Kenny said, looking over at Teme in what could only be described as disgust.

"Yeah, she's not one of us." Peter said with contempt in his voice. "And she has a funny smell to her."

"What are you guys talking about?" Steve asked as if what they were saying made no sense.

"We understand that you're trying to order Chinese take out." Todd said with a chuckle. "We're not trying to prevent you from going to Bang cock!"

"What?" Steve said angrily!

"You know, get in her pants, get a little pussy action and that's cool with us. You just don"t need to bring the gook around here ever again." Kenny said as he again looked over to where Teme was still standing.

Steve turned and walked away from his friends furiously. He could hear his friends saying they'd see him next weekend. When he reached Teme he tried his best not to look angry as he took her hand and led her away from the pond. "Sayonara," his friends screamed out loudly to them as they were leaving.

They hadn't spoken to each other during the whole walk that it took them to reach Union Street. Steve was too busy thinking about what his friends had said about Teme. Even after hearing it, it was still hard for him to grasp the cold hard truth that his friends were racist. What made matters worse was had he not met and fallen in love with Teme would he have behaved like that to someone along with his friends. He highly doubted he'd ever do such a thing, but these were his friends growing up. Whenever they did something it was almost always together. He was serious when he told Teme that he viewed them like brothers instead of just merely friends.

"Are you okay?" Teme asked, breaking the silence between them

"Yeah, yeah, I'm okay. I just got something that I have to do and it's just going to be really hard for me to do!" Steve said sadly.

"Well, if you truly think it's for the best, you should just do it and get it over with." Teme said sadly.

"You're absolutely right." Steve said, stopping Teme and turning her so he could look her straight in the eyes, "I have something that I have to tell you and it can't wait."

"Oh okay!" Teme said, trying to hide the depression in her voice.

"Well, I've decided not to come down this way as much. I was hoping we could spend more time together. That is if you wouldn't mind." Steve said with a sigh.

"I.....No, I wouldn't mind at all." Teme stammered. "I...I'd like that actually."

"Are you okay? You seem kind of rattled." Steve said, concerned. "Is it the cold? Do I need to take you somewhere warm fast?"

"No, I just thought that you were going to say something else." Teme said, trying to hide how happy she was at what Steve actually did say.

"Oh, like what?" Steve asked, looking at her curiously'\.

"I thought you were going to suggest we change our song from faithfully, to that stalker song by the Police." Teme lied.

"What stalker song by the Police, they made a stalker song?" Steve asked, staring at Teme in total disbelief.

"You know the song, the one that says, 'Every breath you take, every move you make, I'll be watching you." Teme said, sort of singing the song more than saying it,

"I love that song. That's the stalker song?" Steve said horrified.

"Just think about the lyrics. They're sort of creepy-ish!" Teme said, faking a shiver.

"I guess it could be a stalker song if you look at it a certain way, but

I'm pretty sure the Police wrote it as a way to say the person was love struck with the other person.Wait, why would you think I'd want to change our song to that?" Steve asked with a puzzled look on his face.

"It's never fun for the hunter when the rabbit has the gun." teme said with a laugh and began to run up the street.

"Oh, you were teasing me!" Steve said as he chased after her.

"Okay, okay, okay!" Teme said, slowing down and trying to catch her breath and Steve wrapped her in his arms. "Let me go! I swear I'll behave!"

"Actually, now that I have you I don't want to let you go. To the victor goes the spoils!" Steve said, pulling her close to him.

"Are you sure Steve? Is this what you really want?" Teme asked as she pulled away from him and looked into his eyes.

"Absolutely!" Steve said.

"I love you!" Teme said, with tears welling in her eyes.

"I love you very much Teme," he said, taking her hand in his and happily continuing their walk home.

HANGING UP THE HELMET

I don't remember how long I sat there with my head resting on the cold metal guard rail. I just remember how good it felt in contrast to my throbbing headache. I'm sure as I lifted my head that there was a red mark across it, but I didn't care. No one would be waiting to interview me anytime soon. My time for the world to care about me was now over. A new face now held the hopes and dreams of my team and fans. My time in the spotlight had sadly come and gone.

The grounds crew were working hard to get the field ready for the game on Sunday. A few of them looked my way and waved once they recognized me. I did a half hearted wave back with a slight nod of my head to them in acknowledgement. I felt the tears running down my face and as I rose from my seat I stood still for a moment without moving to gain composure. I knew that I wasn't crying caused by any pain, but the harsh acceptance of the bitter reality that my career was over. No matter what I did or how hard I begged or prayed, I would never play football again.

I knew a lot of people wouldn't think of that as the end of the world. However, think of the retired police officer or firefighter who listens to their police scanners at night. They remember, and wish they could still be a part of the action. The retired teacher who still tutors. The retired priest or religious leader who still visits people to share their wisdom and knowledge. The parents whose children have all grown up, but constantly reflect on what they taught their children when they were younger. These things become a person's makeup, who they are and for me all I've ever known since I was a little boy was how to play football.

You would think that growing up with a dad who played pro football would be every kid's dream. Well, I can assure you that in some ways it was and in alot of ways it wasn't. As for material wants I had none, but emotionally I was seriously lacking. My dad was the Quarterback for the Massachusetts Minutemen and a father second. When the team had home games it didn't mean the players were actually at home. When I would wake up in the morning my father would already be gone. He would go bright and early to the team's practice facility to watch game films of the opponent. Then he would have to go through the team practice. Now, teams don't necessarily have practice every day. However, to be in game shape players have to go that extra mile and that's a twenty four hour a day process.

Then there's meetings with the television media, the radio media, autograph signings, and personal appearances. So when my dad was able to finally stagger into the house he was so exhausted he would just go to bed.

Now don"t get me wrong, I loved when my dad had home games1 During that time I did get to spend a little time with him. When he was playing in an away game I'd be lucky to speak with him for maybe five minutes a night on the phone.

When home, my dad would leave early on game day, but we wouldn't be far behind. Home games to be honest were incredible. My mother and I would join the other families of players at the stadium.

Usually, the owner had a room with all types of food and drinks for everyone. Then once we were done eating and mingling we'd all head out to the families reserved seats to watch the game. I loved looking around and seeing how full the stadium was. I sometimes would stick out my chest proudly because my dad was the Quarterback, the leader of the team. All these people came here to cheer for my father and watch him lead his team to victory. Now that's truly a feeling only kids growing up with a parent or parents who play pro sports could understand.

Unfortunately, my father, like all of us, is human and didn't always do good. Those times would take my little puffed up chest and totally deflate it. It's just as an overwhelming effect to hear all those people boo your parents as well, but not in a good way. I often look back and laugh about how I would put my hands on my hips and stomp my feet yelling at the crowd, "Stop booing my daddy! You big meanies!" Hey, I was a child and at the time it was the best defense I could muster.

If my fathers team won, we'd all go back to the team's club house and wait for the team to finish showering and changing. Once they were done they'd join us and we had so much fun. Everyone would be laughing and joking. Reporters and family members would be talking to players about plays they made and how good they were. It was one big happy family, but times do change! Some players retire due to injuries. Some players retire because of their age, but the one thing that always remains is the love all players have for the game.

PEE WEE FOOTBALL

My first experience on a football team was in the Pee Wee league. I remember my mom and dad bringing me to Pine Hill Park in the city of Lynn, Massachusetts where we were living at the time. My dad was good friends with the coach of a team called, the Little Warriors. I was so happy to hear how proudly my dad talked to the coach about me. I would often play catch with my dad in the backyard of our house, but to hear him talk he felt I was a natural quarterback.

I'm sure who my dad was and his little talk to his friend was how I actually got to be the Quarterback, but who cares how it happened. It was in the Little Warriors that I gained my love of football.

After school the whole team would meet at the park to have practice.

This was where we all learned the fundamentals of the game. We learned what a playbook was , what the X's and O's stood for, what actually was required of us to become a team. It's also where I learned the pains of working out and how hard it was to get the shoulder pads over my head. I also learned how embarrassing it was to shop for an athletic cup with my mom. I'm not talking about a drinking cup, what I'm talking about is a protective piece used by male athletes to protect a certain area of our body. It's very uncomfortable to wear when you're young, but when you grow older you understand and appreciate its value way more.

Our opening was incredible, we played a team called the Little Spartans. I know a few of their players, because they went to my school. When the game actually started all organization went out the window and it became more of a game of Muckle. I did throw the ball on a couple of plays, but the ball seemed so big in my hands. We ended up losing, but it was so much fun. After the game both went to the concession stand for food and hanging around together. To hear us talk we played like our heroes we watched on television each weekend. I was told how good my passes were and I responded by praising whoever I was speaking to and telling that person how good they did at their position. We all laughed and joked with one another until it was finally time to leave.

Due to the fact that my games were on the weekends my dad couldn't come and watch me play. My mom would videotape the games and he would watch them when he came home. When he was done watching them he would always sit me down and point out the things to me that he thought I could do better. My dad wasn't one of those psycho parents who screamed and yelled if their child didn't play well. Honestly, he would always end our conversations by saying, "Son, just go out there and enjoy yourself. That's all that truly matters." That's how I've always played the game, because that's how it was meant to be played.

Our playoffs were not played at Pine Hill Park, but at Manning Bowl Stadium. This was where the highschool teams played, so you can imagine how awed we felt to be playing in an actual stadium. Every team made the playoffs and the games started on Friday after school and ended on Sunday. The Little Warriors finished our first season in fifth place. Which wouldn't be too bad, but we only had eight teams in the league. We all got to go to a league banquet, held at a local pizza parlor and every player received a trophy. So when I went to show my father the trophy I received, I did it with a proud heart.He ran his hand through my hair messing it up and told me to keep up the good work. My dad took that trophy and put it in his trophy case and later on bought me my very own trophy case to fill.

I continued the football journey as I grew older to Pop Warner Football and then to Junior High School football. This is when the playbook becomes more complicated and becoming more physically fit is vital to your development as a player. It's also when you become more concerned with wins, loses, and personal statistics.

HIGH SCHOOL FOOTBALL

My freshman year at Lynn English High School was both fun and depressing. It would be my family's last year in Lynn, Massachusetts. My dad had finally retired from pro football and decided to focus on my future.

He made up his mind that it would be better for me to show off my talents as a Quarterback in a school where I could win a state championship and get media attention. Unfortunately, he felt that would be in Dallas, Texas. Despite my pleas for him to reconsider and allow me to stay with my friends, on this matter he had his mind firmly made up.

I decided it would be best not to tell my teammates until the year was over. Which turned out to be the best decision, because without that distraction we ended up only losing one game that year. I spent a lot of time that year at Lynn Beach walking along the sea wall. There's a ledge that runs along the wall and in some places it gets really narrow and hard to walk. The thing is, at high tide you have to try and dodge the waves as they come in and crash upon the wall. If you do get hit by a wave you have to brace yourself against the wall and hope the wave doesn't drag you off the ledge and into the ocean. The smaller waves do push you back to the ledge so you can get back up before the larger ones hit, but it's extremely scary. I look back on this now and realize how foolish and dangerous it really was, but back then it was a test of bravery and skill. To me it was the challenge of making it along the whole ledge without getting totally soaked. I guess that's how I view football, it's the thrill and the challenge. The determination to be better than the team you face each week, to be the best. They were the waves that wanted to prevent me from making it to my final destination and I would not allow them to pull me off my course.

We moved over the summer and I can still see my friends' faces, as they helped me load the moving van. We laughed and joked, but the hurt and disbelief that I was going to be gone was plainly visible on their faces. I'm sure they could read it on my face as well. Hell, we didn't only have football memories together. These were the people I had associated with my whole life so far. We used to rub sticks in dog poop and chase each other around. We made forts out of all sorts of discarded items and fought off imaginary invaders. We used to tell each other how icky and yucky girls were. Then when we got older we kicked ourselves for not realizing how awesome girls truly were.

When the van pulled away I almost broke my neck trying to look back. I saw my friends chasing after the van, but when we turned left at the corner they were gone. It was all gone, everything I'd ever known, and now only memories remained.

TEXAS

"Everything's Bigger In Texas," that's the saying, and believe me it is very true. The expectations were big, the players were big, and the media coverage of football was huge. It seems my dad wasn't the only former player who brought his son to play here in Texas. To be honest, it was a virtual High School All Star Team that was assembled here. The coach was a football legend and had coached here for years.

Had actually coached many of the players' dads that were here, including my dad. We were provided the best equipment and uniforms money could buy. These were donations from local businessmen who would come watch us practice and see our games. I just want to say that if a person owns a cattle ranch or oil company and donates to your High School Football Team, trust me you'll know.

Truthfully, I was nervous being in a new situation, but we all were from other states, except six players, so we bonded fairly quickly. That's the good part of being on a team. You have to practice and go to war together, which causes you to gel together faster. We spent a lot of time talking about our home towns, teams we played on, games that stood out, and things we used to do for fun.

We had two teammates from Texas that talked us into going to see a rodeo. I being from Massachusetts had never been to a rodeo and had an amazing time. Then as it got later they talked us into going cow tipping. I never knew cows slept while standing up or why my teammates thought it was funny to push them over while they slept. I did learn that I was an extremely fast runner when being chased by a man holding a shotgun.

On the field our offense and defense were things of beauty. Now off the field as individuals many of us were a total mess. I was always careful about my drinking or putting myself into situations that would come back to haunt me later on. I think that was one thing my dad drilled into my head. "Things will come back on you! No matter how small you think they are, someone will hold it against you!" I saw that first hand with many of my teammates who got in trouble with the law. A lot of times the players would be giving breaks so as not to hurt their careers, but sometimes the media would get wind of it before anyone could sweep it under the rug. When that happened many of the better colleges passed on them when it came to recruiting. Always remember, image is everything!

I was sitting at a table with three hats in front of me and media cameras everywhere I looked. The hat that I chose to pick up would be the college I decided to commit myself too. There was LSU, Alabama, and Florida. But the one I truly wanted to go to was not an option. I really wanted to go to USC, but my dad talked me out of it. When we talked about potential colleges I immediately said, "USC!" He just simply looked at me calmly and asked, "Why?" I rambled off about the beaches, the girls in bikinis, movie stars, and visiting DisneyLand. That's when he looked at me and replied, "You haven't mentioned what type of education you'd receive. The positives and negatives of the football program there, or how going there will help you reach your dream of turning pro." So in the end he talked me into the three teams who's hats sat before me now. All of them were in the SEC, and he had a good reason behind that decision. In college football the SEC is probably the best conference and has the most televised games. These three schools also offered more of what I was seeking educational wise as well. I know a lot of football players are pushed through school, but that never happened to me. I sometimes wish it had, but all in all I'm truly glad it didn't.

So there I sat and when it came time I moved my hand over all the hats for a dramatic effect. Then I grabbed the Florida hat and placed it on my head. There was a loud cheer and alot of hand shaking and pats on the back for congratulations. My dad hugged me tight and said, "You don't fool me. Florida has beaches, girls in bikinis, movie stars, and Disney World!" Which caused us both to laugh out loud and draw weird stares from the people around us. When my mom came over to me I began to cry. It dawned on me that I was going to be going away to college. I would no longer see this wonderful woman everyday. She had been there for me through thick and thin all these years. She had driven me and my teammates throughout the years to practices, games, and other places since I was a little boy. I Owed her so much and I promised to do my best to make her proud.

The summer after I graduated from highschool was spent preparing for my departure to college. My dad had obtained the playbooks for Florida and we studied it diligently. When I wasn't studying the playbook I was packing my belongings. My mom often helped me pack and always had tears in her eyes. These moments always ended up with us hugging one another and her telling me, "Be good and make sure you behave yourself."

The thought of leaving Texas and the friends I made on the team didn't affect me as much as when I left Lynn. I think that it had a lot to do with the fact I was brought to do good and move on to better my chances to turn pro. Whereas when I left Lynn it was more of a surprise. I realized when we went over colleges that I never once thought of choosing one in Massachusetts. Yet when I was younger that was all I dreamed of. I wanted to play for a local college and be the hometown hero. That's the one thing you realize as you grow older. The dream may be the same. But the path you take to get there is most likely going to change.

FLORIDA

If you have never had the chance to go to college, you truly missed out on one of the best experiences of a lifetime. Especially if you happen to play for one of the school teams. In highschool we were looked at as being one of the cool kids and it was a greatest feeling. In college you are placed on a pedestal and viewed as demigods. The whole school revels in your wins and feels the pain of your losses.

When you're walking to your classes, it seems like everyone wants to talk to you or wish you the best come game time. In some cases you can see the worship in their eyes. This struck me as odd my freshman year because I didn't even play in a game yet. All the other students knew was that the recruiters believed in me and if that was the case, so did they. Now it's easy to get caught up in all the partying and fun that goes along with college life, but beyond foolish if you're an athlete. Once again reputation is everything and mistakes will follow you and in some cases end your professional career before it ever starts.

I enrolled in classes that were considered to be very hard. I must admit between the playbook and my homework I often found myself feeling overwhelmed. I had teammates who took what were called cake classes and didn't take college seriously. For me, I knew better, my dad always told me school first and football second. He would remind me that someday I would no longer be playing football and when that day came what would I do without a proper education to fall back on. "Don't be one of those players who squanders their money thinking football is going to last forever. Only to wake up one day and it's over and you have nothing to fall back on and waste your life." he would say.

One thing I found to be difficult was traveling to different states to play games and having to do homework and study the playbook. Having done this, it is my belief college students keep the caffeine pill industry in business. On Sunday the day after the games were played you'd think we'd be able to rest. Well, someone would always rush into the dorm rooms or hotel rooms with the newspaper. It didn't matter what newspaper or magazine it was, if it had our names or photos in it, it would be waved in our faces. We'd either be congratulated on how the article portrayed us or talk trash about whoever wrote bad reviews of our playing.

When the media finally started recognizing me as someone the fans wanted to hear more about this cut into my personal time even more. Now not only was I juggling time between homework and the playbook. Now I had to find time to sit down and do interviews with the media. Unfortunately, giving interviews is a must for any athlete. You do not want to be labeled as someone who is not media friendly. At least not when you're first trying to break into professional sports, maybe once you get in, but never before. As I will keep saying. " Image is everything!"

Through all this we have to try and find time to balance a social life as well. I was in highschool when my dad rented a movie called, An Officer and A Gentleman. In the movie a blonde girl wants to get pregnant on purpose in order to marry a cadet so she is financially secure and sees the world. My dad stopped the movie at that part and said. "Son, you're going to have girls literally throwing themselves at you in the hopes of getting pregnant. They're called Gold Diggers. They only love the idea of your money and what they can get out of you. So, please find yourself a good person who doesn't like football, never heard of you, and likes you for you!"

Now my dad was one hundred percent right about these girls. The one thing my dad didn't tell me was a lot of these girls could have been Playboy centerfolds. I would be lying if I told you that I never gave into the temptation. I was smart enough to wear protection during those weak moments and thankfully never suffered any repercussions from them. I can't say the same for some of my teammates though. I've seen some who moved on to the professional level and have four or five baby mothers. Many more are trapped in bad marriages where either they or their wife is constantly cheating.

I was lucky to actually meet a girl like the one my dad had suggested for me. We married after we graduated from college. When we first met though she wanted nothing to do with me. Like most people she thought I was a jock who was getting a free ride through college because I could play football. Until she learned that I was a dedicated student with good grades who had no intentions of leaving school early to enter the NFL Draft. Then and only then did she agree to go on a date with me and we've been together ever since.

Declaring early to enter the NFL Draft is what a lot of college players do and in no way are they truly ready to be in the NFL. This also puts a lot of pressure on the players who are staying at the college level. What I mean is with teammates graduating, transferring, declaring for the NFL Draft, the team is in a constant form of change. Each year the faces and names are going to change on the team, This is also true when it comes to the talent level. In some cases the new player may be better than the one who departed and in other cases the player may be a downgrade. This is where the talent scouts and coaches have to do their part and earn their money. They have to assemble a team that in all honesty has a legitimate chance at winning a National Title each year.

I mentioned before about how donations to high schools bought the best equipment and uniforms. Well, donations by college boosters dwarf them by a long shot! They don't only donate money, they build whole buildings for the college. They do a lot of good, but can also be the death of football careers. To motivate players they may offer them a new car, give them spending money, or buy a house for their family. Let's be honest, a player who's grown up in poverty or seen their family suffer is most likely going to accept the gifts. Especially if their family is in desperate need and they can save them immediately with a boosters gift. However, once it gets out that a player took money or gifts it's a black mark against them and the college. The player could be deemed academically unable to play or in most instances expelled and ruining their chance to go Pro. The colleges usually have to pay fines, have sanctions set against them, and can even lose Bowl eligibility. Which in a way is a devastating blow to the college financially.

I feel that there are three major games to be played in college football. The first would be the Homecoming Game. This is an event for the whole school and makes you truly swell with school pride. I can't begin to explain the fun and excitement you feel at your college's Pep Rally.

You have practically the whole college there chanting the college fight song and screaming for you to achieve victory over your opponent, it's an incredible adrenaline rush. The second would be the College Division Championship game. At the end of the season this is where you want to be, preparing for this game. When the dust settles and the final whistle blows you want to be the team that walks back onto its college campus as Division Champions. It's an amazing feeling to see the pride in your fellow students' faces knowing their school is one of the best in the nation.

Which brings me to the game that declares who is the absolute best in the nation, the National Championship! No one who ever played college football can honestly look you in the face and say they had no desire to be a National Champion.

It's one thing to have your college classmates recognize your achievements on the football field, but to win it all and have the whole nation know that your college is the cream of the crop is a totally different experience. It is by far the ultimate feeling to step out into the stadium to play on national television to be recognized if you win as the all around best in the country.

I was lucky enough to play in two National Championship games. The first was my junior year and we ended up losing that game by only a field goal. You can not imagine how devastated we were. On the trip back to our college many of us were crying and hugged our teammates who were graduating and would never have the chance again to play for the National Championship.

That's why it's such a monumental moment, because with the team constantly changing you don't know if you'll ever get there again. So you want to go out there and win it all when you have the opportunity. Unfortunately, the other team has the same mind set and only one team can win and it wasn't us that year. We ended up going back again the next year to again play for the National Championship and won by ten points. This meant so much to me because it was my senior year of college and our team ended up finishing at the very top of the mountain. The celebration was incredible, we were in a parade, and the whole state seemed to come out to celebrate our victory. I've never seen such a turn out before in my whole life. It made me want to work even harder to achieve even greater moments whenI reached the professional level.

In high school I was tackled a few times and had what they call the wind knocked out of me. While playing college ball I had what was called my bell rung a few times. I remember one of the first times it happened. I was plastered by a Linebacker and my Lineman grabbed the front of my jersey and pulled me to my feet. I looked at him and said, "I see three of you." He just smiled and said, "Well, when you throw to the Receiver, target the one in the middle." I shook my head trying to clear the cobwebs and asked, "Will the guy in the middle catch it?" He laughed real loud and said, "He's either going to catch it and turn you into a hero, or the defense intercepts it and you become the most hated player on campus."

The Receiver did catch the ball that day, but I mention this event for another reason. I did not realize just how much damage was being done to my body from these hits. I guess it could be construed to cause and effect. If an extremely large Linebacker wraps his arms around me and causes me to be driven to the ground as hard as he possibly can. The effect can be any number of things. Such as having my bell rung, torn muscles, broken bones, concussions, or years later lingering medical issues from the repeated abuse.

You hear people say, "He's seeing stars!" Well, those are mild or slight concussions. At first they seem like nothing, but those hits add up and in the end the price your body pays is a debt that will be with you the rest of your life. What happens is you don't go over to the sidelines after one of these hits no matter how you feel. Because you don't want to gain the reputation as someone who can't take a hit. When it happened I would usually roll onto my hands and knees and punch the ground a few times to help me regain my bearings so I could stand. I didn't take too much time with this because I didn't want the Referees to get concerned. So on numerous occasions I was still dazed as I entered the huddle.

Honestly, sometimes I didn't even remember what play I called or how I even completed it because I was so out of it. I had two games in college where I was hit and didn't remember even playing the game or anything after it when Im woke up the next morning. I watched tapes of the games and wondered who was controlling my body, because as far as I knew I wasn't.

I knew a guy in college who would drink so much he'd go into a blackout. You'd have conversations with him, he'd walk and fill his cup, but in the morning he wouldn't remember any of it. We used to laugh and say, "The lights were on, but nobody was home!" That was until I experienced my first blackout then I didn't think his situation was funny anymore. In fact, it scared the hell out of me, but I didn't tell anyone. I didn't want to risk the chance of being told that I couldn't play football anymore. I know now that it was wrong and all I did was hurt myself. I understand that now, but at the time I was young and in my mind indestructible. I was going to be fine, all I had to do was work harder and I'd be fine.

I was nominated for the Heisman Trophy my senior year. I didn't win, but it was fun going to the presentation ceremony. I was very disappointed in losing, but just being nominated is something special. When I talked to my dad he was very proud of the fact that I had been nominated. He also told me not to be too disappointed because winning the Heisman Trophy didn't mean you'd move on to the NFL and have a great career. There were many Heisman winners who went to the NFL and were a bust.

My dad hired an agent that he knew to help me with my professional career. Now my personal opinion of agents isn't a good one. For me I few them as new car sales when it comes to representing college players. At first it's as if they are selling a Ferrari. Now here we have this sleek new Quarterback with a very accurate throw, who can also throw the deep pass. He comes from a good pedigree, with his father who played Quarterback at the professional level. He's won a National Championship and was a runner up to the prestigious Heisman Trophy. So make an offer that will knock our socks off and he's yours. Then when you've been in the league for awhile or retired they morph into used car salesmen. That's when the effort to sell you becomes minimal. They are too focused on the new you coming out of college, because that's where the big money is. I've witnessed this first hand between my dad and his longtime agent. I sat and listened to my dad on numerous occasions argue with his agent about autograph signings and other low paying appearances. I give a lot of credit to my dad because of all the sound advice he's given me to help me deal with all these problems. He wisely advised me that when I did sign my contract to not get caught up in spending the money foolishly. He said something that made a ton of sense. It's not true that he who has the most toys wins. It's he who still can buy toys at the end of their career that truly wins. I've sadly seen many football players at the end of their careers flat broke. So I can say that what he was telling me was rock solid advice.

The summer after my senior year of college was very overwhelming. My girlfriend and I decided to get married. Which was the best decision of my life. If you are lucky enough to find a good partner then you'd be an idiot if you didn't keep them. Especially nowadays when a good partner is almost impossible to find. Then I had to attend an NFL Pro day. The players that are considered to be drafted by an NFL team are gathered together to show off what they can do physically and at their football positions. This consisted of me throwing the football, and numerous other tests. This was all done to show off my quarterbacking abilities to the professional scouts. I actually could not tell you how many interviews I actually had with the media. While all this was going on my agent was running around like a chicken with his head cut off. I found myself reading every magazine and newspaper to see what was being said about me. I also listened and watched the sports channels every chance I could. In truth I was a nervous wreck through all of it.

When everything was said and done I went to New York to attend the NFL Draft. I had been to New York on a few occasions with my parents when I was younger. So I became the unofficial guide for the other draft players throughout the city. I was already overwhelmed by everything that was going on, so being in a familiar city took some pressure off.

I had numerous interviews at the NFL Pro Day with different coaches and team officials from many NFL teams. They all showed some inter- est in possibly drafting me. When I spoke with my agent he told me not to worry he had it all under control. He did ask me if I preferred to play in hot weather or cold. Then he also asked me if I enjoyed living in big cities or small. He did tell me that it was highly possible for me to be a top ten pick. The Heisman Trophy winner had some off field problems and caused it to drop his draft value. Which of course in turn caused my draft value to rise!

On the night of the Draft we were brought into the Green room to wait for our names to be called. There were twenty five of us and we were all predicted to be selected in the first round.I knew that being in this room didn't guarantee that, some sitting here could be in for a disappointment. I just hoped that I wouldn't be one of those still sitting here after the first round closed with my name not called in disappointment. I realized that it truly didn't matter what round I was drafted in, I was about to fulfill something I had dreamed of my whole life.

As I watched and listened to each team make their selection I was becoming a nervous wreck. I hugged and congratulated each player as their name was called. We watched them go to the podium and hold up their new team jerseys. When Los Angeles picked at number eight they selected me. I was truly in a state of shock and awe when my name was called. Los Angeles wasn't even a team I had spoken with at my Pro Day. I had no idea that they were even interested in me at all. I received hand shakes and pats on the back as I made my walk to the podium. I don't think there are words to describe the feeling you get when you're standing there and the NFL Commissioner shakes your hand and gives you your new team's Jersey. Your heart fills with so much pride as you realize you have officially become a Professional Football Player.

LOS ANGELES

My agent worked out my contract details with the team. I must admit he made it so the team was going to pay me a decent amount of money under my rookie contract for three years. My wife and I bought a nice house not too far away from the team facility. I remember my new teammates asking me why I didn't buy a mansion and hire servants. I would just tell them that I had other plans for the money at the moment. Which to be honest, we really did! We invested in different stocks and bonds, a fast food franchise, and bought some property in Kentucky that had development potential. I also donated some money to various charities, many professional athletes donate money and their time to the charities they support. You'll hear a lot of people say that we only do it for the tax write offs or the publicity. In some cases who knows that may be correct, but many players actually donate because they truly care.

I had some time before I had to report to the OTA's, so my wife and I decided to explore our new city. I have to say, Los Angeles is everything I thought it would be and more. While we were taking in the sites by day at night I was studying the teams playbook. MY agent was constantly calling to tell me of different product endorsements and interviews he was setting up for me, I realized while college was hard in its own ways. It was nothing compared to the requirements I now faced as a NFL product. I was literally being pulled in one hundred different directions and I wasn't even playing the game yet!

The one thing you learn is that any team that picks early in the draft has numerous needs. Unfortunately, Los Angeles had alot of needs to fill. I was supposed to spend my first year or two watching and learning behind a veteran quarterback. Well, in our first game of the season he got carted off the field injured, so they put me in. I spent that game and basically the rest of that season running for my life.

I spent most of my rookie year bruised, battered, and bandaged! When my wife told me we were expecting our first child I jumped for joy. Well, as beat up as I was it was more of a calf raise and groan. I think my wife is truly the most patient person in the world. She would wrap my bruised body and rub creams into my aches. I have to admit through it all she was amazing. She used to just smile at me and say, "In for a dime, in for a dollar!" That's when you know you have a good wife if you play professional sports. They're there for you through thick and thin! The second to last game of the season I was knocked into the twilight zone. When I woke up in the hospital there beside my bed was my wife and my agent. My wife was an emotional basket case and my agent was making sure his investment would be okay. That was my first medically diagnosed concussion, but we all know I had plenty before this. From what I'm told, after the hit when the coaching and medical staff asked me who I was I replied. "Yes, I'm Batman!" I laugh at this now, but to be honest it isn't funny.

That was pretty much my first three years in Los Angeles. The General Manager and coaches would always tell me they were going to address the offensive line issues through free agency and the draft. Yet every year despite their efforts the offensive line never got better and the bruises and broken bones increased. I suffered my second diagnosed concussion my third and final year in Los Angeles. While I was recovering I asked my wife if she would be disappointed if I chose to sign with another team and we had to move. I thought for sure that she wouldn't even consider it since she was involved in different projects in the area. I was shocked when she started naming possible teams and cities to go to. She told me that it was tearing her up inside seeing me banged up constantly. She knew that marrying a football player she'd have to deal with bruises and dings, but this was getting ridiculous. So as the season came to a close I told my agent to start exploring other options. I had gained the reputation of being a gamer. If I got knocked down I'd pick myself up and get back in the game no matter what. Having that type of reputation actually got me a lot of looks from many different teams.

I traveled to a few other team facilities and tried out for their coaching staff. I actually enjoyed all the visits and the V.I.P. treatment each team gave me. The one that stuck out the most was Massachusetts though. That was where my dad played his professional career and I had so many fond memories. I didn't want to make any decision without first consulting my wife, but she was the one who told me she hoped I'd choose the Massachusetts team. When I asked her why, she told me that she wanted to see snow and experience the change of the seasons. She wanted to see the leaves on the trees change color and go apple picking. Then there was my son's education to consider. The school systems in Massachusetts are some of the best in the country. Our son getting a good education was a big factor in her decision. So taking all that into consideration I agreed to sign a four year deal with Massachusetts and leave Los Angeles.

When someone asks me to think of one game that stands out in my mind, I truly can't. What stands out in my mind are the friendships and camaraderie you build on the teams you play for. We would play pranks on one another and share family moments together. When my dad played teams stayed together longer than they do today. Now teams are constantly changing and it's totally different. What's not different is the emotions you share as teammates. Those feelings no matter what team you play for will never change.

MASSACHUSETTS

My dad was ecstatic about me playing for his old team. He explained what it was going to be like playing at the teams stadium. To him it was in a way of me actually following in his footsteps. I was glad to see that my decision made him happy and I hoped I could live up to his expectations. He couldn't stay away from football after he retired and was a sports commentator on a sports network. So he'd be covering my games sometimes and asked the network if he could relocate to the Massachusetts branch.

He told me that he and my mom were getting bored in Florida and were thinking of moving back to Massachusetts anyway. He told me Florida was either for the really young or really old and they were neither. I knew that the real reason they wanted to do this was to be closer to their grandson, but just laughed when he told me these reasons.

We bought a house in Newburyport, but I brought my wife on a tour of Lynn to show her where I grew up. I showed her the ledge along the seawall that I used to walk in highschool. She gave me a weird look and asked me if I was insane. Which brought a big smile to my face because only an insane person would play an insane person would do what I do for a living! We drove by my old house and Lynn English. The more places we visited, the more I felt at home.

I've had people tell me that I never had a real job, all I did was play a game and get over paid to play it. I argue that I was hired to do a job and I have to live up to the expectations and responsibilities that come with it. I had to go to practice, study game film, learn and execute the playbook, and be a spokesperson for the team. Now I'm not asking anyone to feel sorry for me or anything to that nature. I understand that as a football player I have advantages other people don't have. However, we deal with a lot of issues the general public doesn't. We have teammates and employees with personal issues they are going through which affects our jobs. Many don't even take their jobs seriouslyThen we have the ones who push themselves harder than their teammates, but make less than most. The general public would be shocked to learn that the same things they go through on a daily basis we also go through on a daily basis. We just deal with it on a different level than most.

I was asked once to explain the feeling of being on a football team. Have you ever heard of the Spartans, Romans, Greeks, or Phoenicians?

Their armies fought battles and deployed shield walls. The two opposing armies would lock shields and push and stab one another to gain ground in battle. The soul purpose of this is to be stronger, fiercer, and be able to vanquish your foe. That's Football! We put on our equipment/armor and go out on the playing field and do battle. We are a team/army and not one individual player/soldier wants to be the cause of our defeat to the enemy. That's why you see players do their best to walk off an injury or lie to the coaching staff about how hurt they are so they can get back in the game/war. You want your enemies to shake their heads in disbelief as you trot back onto the field after you took a vicious hit. You want to see the fear in their eyes as momentum shifts and you're forcing them back towards their own goal line. There's truly no greater feeling than helping your team/army rally from what seemed like a certain defeat to a tremendous victory. Unfortunately, that also can happen with the other team/army in a game/battle. The thing is each week's game/battle takes on a life of its own. Heroes are created on both sides of the opposing teams/armies, and are either victorious or suffer the bitter taste of defeat. Each week these heroes are asked to take on new challenges and make their fans/people proud. For me it's as if I'm living Homer's Iliad and returning home to the jubilations of my fans/people, I always enjoyed a great war story.

I had a great time playing in my home state of Massachusetts and I played some of the best football of my career there. I still came home with my body bruised and saw stars a few times. I will say that it was nowhere even close to the amount I experienced in Los Angeles though. We made it to the playoffs in my second year on the team. This was my first time as a professional football player making it to the playoffs, so I soaked it all in. It was refreshing to have the media focus on how well the team was doing and that our success was a total team effort. It also felt good to give our fans a winning season. We did lose in the second round of the playoffs, but it was a sure sign of better things to come. At least that was the hope! The Universe must have heard us say that and had an answer for us. In the third game of the following season I tore my ACL in the second quarter of the game. I ended up having to sit out the rest of the season rehabbing the injury. I was beyond frustrated at my luck especially after the year we had the last season. This made me work extra hard in my physical therapies to strengthen my leg and get back to the team after I had my surgery. I did get to spend a lot of time with my wife and son, so there was an upside. When I returned the next year it was the final year of the four year contract I had signed with the team. We were having an incredible season and the whole team was talking about us reaching the playoffs and going to the Super Bowl. Then with three games left in the season I got blindsided by a linebacker who got by my Left Tackle. When the medical staff asked me if I knew who I was, I was told by many of the coaches and my teammates that I replied, "Of Course, I'm Batman!" When I woke up in the hospital I truly had no idea how I got there. The concerned looks that my wife and agent had on their faces worried me. I was told when the doctor came in to see me that I had suffered a severe concussion. I would have to go through a series of tests before he would even consider allowing me to play football again. He did finally clear me to play and I'm glad he did because the team had made it to the Superbowl!

At the beginning of every year every team has aspirations of making it to the Superbowl, but in the end only two teams get to walk onto the field to compete. Some players have never made it to this game in their whole careers. So to be here is an honor and testament to the hard work and dedication the team put in this year. The whole week before the game is a media frenzy, interviews and pictures, it's truly a circus. I can't even begin to tell you how many conversations I ended up having or questions I answered before the big game. In the end when the dust had cleared and the game was played, we ended up losing, and the feeling was awful! The confetti is falling all around you, the opposing team is celebrating and presented with the Lombardi Trophy. Which is the Holy Grail of Football, the one thing every player seeks and gives their all every year they play to claim it. I have to admit this was one of the saddest days of my life and still hurts to this day. To be that close and have it just slip through your fingers is a gut wrenching experience. However, that was not the absolute worst thing to ever happen to me, that was coming soon.

I didn't even consider exploring other teams when I became a free agent. I had my agent work out another deal with Massachusetts. I had decided that this was the organization that I wanted to play for and eventually retire with. I honestly believed that I would finish this new four year contract and in the end see if I still wanted to play or walk away from the game. The problem with that is things hardly ever turn out how you plan them out, this is a sad lesson we learn in life.

It was the last game of the preseason and I had no business trying to run and gain a first down. The game was meaningless and I have no clue what I was thinking of putting myself in that situation. As I started to run I saw the linebacker bearing down on me. I should have attempted to slide, but instead I threw my body forward to reach the first down marker. I don't remember anything after that moment. I've been told that the hit on me looked brutal and I helicopter spinned in the air before I crashed to the ground short of the first down. I have yet to this day watched any footage of the play because of repercussions that followed it. I ended up being carted off the field unconscious to the horror of my family who were in the stands for the game. I don't believe any player would want to watch an experience like that over and over again.

When I woke up in the hospital it was like experiencing deja vu.

There was my wife and agent sitting by my bedside waiting for me to wake up. The only thing different about this time was that my mom and dad were there as well. When the doctor finally walked inI smiled at him and said, "Let me guess I had another severe concussion." He did not smile and kindly asked everyone to leave the room so he could talk to me in private. I told him whatever he had to say to me he could say in front of everyone in the room. He explained that the x-rays showed that I had experienced too many concussions in my career and that if I experienced another I could either die or become paralyzed. He could not in good faith as my doctor allow me to play football ever again. I remember yelling at him and crying and just the ton of emotions his words caused to rush over me. I demanded a second opinion and asked if he got his Doctor's degree from a Cracker Jack box! I'm pretty sure I said way more insults about him, his past generations and future generations in my anger. He never lost his composure at my outburst and said he was sure I could find another Doctor to sign the okay for me to play, but to think of the consequences.

When he left the room there was a lot more crying and hugging as we faced this diagnosis. My family was very clear that they wanted me to listen to the doctor and not play Russian Roulette with my life by trying to go back on the football field. The thought of me not participating or ever seeing my son grow up was the driving force in me accepting the Doctors decision. I have to admit my agent was even teary eyed, I want to believe it was because of what had happened and not us having to walk away from the money on the contract I just signed. I have heard of agents and clients becoming good friends during their time together. I however cannot but stick by my view of them as a high priced car salesman and his porsche just got forced to the junk pile.

I've been asked if at a young age had anyone ever taken me aside and told me the dangers of playing football. As a player and a fan who both participated and watched football you can"t help but know the risk. I can't begin to tell you how many times I've seen or heard of players suffering season ending or career ending injuries. The thing is playing Professional Football was my childhood dream, and nothing and no one was going to stop me from achieving it. As a player you get it in your head that the injuries you hear other players suffered and ended their careers won't happen to you. Then there's the inner voice also telling you that any injury you sustain can be overcome by pushing yourself harder and focusing on returning to the football field. It's hard to admit that you're mortal when for as long as you can remember you pushed yourself to be stronger and faster than everyone around you.

PRESENT DAY

A week after my release from the hospital I returned to the team facility. When I walked into the locker room for some strange reason I remembered a verse from the bible, Matthew 6:34. "Therefore do not worry about tomorrow, for tomorrow will worry about itself. Each day has enough trouble of its own." I laughed at how true that verse is as I walked over to my locker and removed my helmet from its peg. I don't know why exactly but I carried it with me into the coaches office. I thought for sure he was going to ask me what I was doing with my helmet, but he never did. The conversation was long and emotional, we talked about the team, how far we had come, and my career. The conversation was more or less me coming to grips with the hard truth that my childhood dream was over. When I left his office I walked back to my locker and placed my helmet back on its peg. Hanging up my helmet after every game was like second nature to me and it just seemed like the right thing to do now that the game was over for me permanently.

As I made my way up the stadium stairs to the exit I remembered an article in a magazine I once read. It was about couples who have spent their whole lives together then sadly one passes away. The remaining spouse has a hard time dealing with the loss because the other person was such a big part of their lives. They end up suffering from severe depression, become seclusive and some even attempt suicide. I've heard it called Survivors Guilt and some have said it's Separation Anxiety, I honestly don't know the exact name for it.

I honestly believe that a form of this affects professional athletes once they're playing days are over. "You can take the player out of the game, but you can't take the game out of the player!" For many of us the sport we play is all we've ever known our whole lives. It has become a major part of our being, it's literally who we are and what we do day in and day out. It's what makes us who we are and when we can no longer do it, what have we become!

I think that's why so many retired players take up coaching, sports announcing, radio shows and other trades connected to the sport they dedicated their whole lives to. It's their way of still being relevant to the sport that is still a big part of them. The thing about that is I don't care what they do because it's not the same. Nothing can take the place of gearing up with your teammates to take the field and do battle each week. For the people who only watch the sports they can never truly understand this feeling. For the ones who have felt this feeling and know its power, nothing we could ever do after it's gone from us could ever compare.

THE WHEEZER

She could feel the sweat running down her back. The vinyl jogging suit was sticking to her body. She was seeing spots before her eyes and gasping for air. The elderly woman was only a few feet away from her, but it didn't matter; she needed her inhaler. She staggered off the jogging path and eased herself onto the park bench. As she struggled to open her fanny pack for her inhaler, she almost cut herself on the steak knife inside. Her hands were shaking as she put the inhaler to her mouth and took two deep puffs. She felt the medicine going to work on her lungs immediately, and her breathing returning to normal. She could still see the elderly jogger through her watering eyes, and cursed to herself in frustration. All her life asthma had prevented her from succeeding. Yet, this idea had seemed perfect when she thought it up. She was sure that becoming a serial killer was the one thing asthma couldn't possibly prevent her from succeeding at. However, the primary target of most serial killers was joggers. Therein lay her problem: not only did her attempt at jogging trigger her asthma, but another problem would have occurred. Had she managed to assault the elderly jogger in a secluded area, she probably would have got her ass kicked and arrested.

All this planning, and the only thing she had accomplished was another failure. She had been so confident when she went and bought her jogging suit. She was even happy to buy a pair of pink and gray Nikes that matched her suit. She told herself just because she was resorting to a life of crime didn't mean she couldn't do it in style.

Then, there was the brilliant idea about the steak knives. She had purchased a number of true detective magazines to research her newest profession. What she had learned was that serial killers that got caught made really stupid mistakes. The most common mistake was using some rare weapon, that some way or another could be traced back to the owner. That caused her to really think about her choice of murder weapon. When she was contemplating this dilemma, she had been in the process of shopping. That's when she walked by the kitchen department and had a brainstorm. Hell, how many households across the United States owned steak knives? Good luck, Mr. Officer-man, tracing this murder weapon, she thought to herself as she made her purchase.

She stared from the bench as another elderly jogger wearing a white suit passed by her. This old bat had the nerve to twiddle her fingers at her. She would have loved to carve that smile off her arrogant little face, and could have if she didn't suffer from this stupid affliction.How come when she was just a little girl playing at the park life seemed so much better? When she had an asthma attack, none of the other kids teased her. The other children would even race to get her parents when she had one. Then, after she used her inhaler and sat for a while, the other children would beg her parents to let her come back and play. Those were the happiest days of her life.Then came the first day of kindergarten. The days leading up to school were great. Her parents took her shopping for school clothes and supplies. The store they shopped at had the coolest lunch pail. It was a " Pretty Princess" design with a built-in thermos. Everything was going so good, until her first recess. That's when she had her first experience with kickball. When it was her turn, she kicked the ball and started to run to first base. Unfortunately, that happened to trigger an attack. That was the day all the names started: "Norma No-Breath," "Puffing Princess," and "Wheezy." Unlike the children at the park, the children throughout her years in elementary school tormented her. She was never picked to play on any team, and spent a lot of time sitting by herself. Her parents always told her the other children would grow out of it, but they never did. Truth be told, they got worse.

Once Norma entered junior high, she was sure things would change for the better. Many of the children she had gone to school with would be going to other schools. She highly doubted that the immaturity in elementary school would follow her to junior high. She was actually having a good first day until she went to Physical Education. The moment she walked into the gym, a girl named Laura Coogan recognized her. Laura began to tease her and call her those old nicknames. Norma was so embarrassed that she ran out with tears in her eyes. The only good thing to come out of this situation was that she was allowed to change her P.E. class to Study Hall due to her asthma. That didn't stop Laura and her buddies from teasing her in the hallways, or at lunch, or on the bus home. If Laura Coogan was one of those joggers passing by, Norma would try her hardest to run her down and plunge that steak knife in her stinking, perfect little neck of hers. It may be the last thing Norma ever did, but it would be so satisfying; it would be worth the consequences. The sight of that blonde-haired, blue-eyed bimbo gasping for air after all the times she made fun of Norma would be classic.

Norma remembered her first experience at killing something during her last year in junior high. Her parents had decided to buy a dog. She had pleaded for a Dalmatian puppy, but her parents were just going to the Humane Society and choosing from whatever they had. Norma was so excited the day they finally went. Her imagination was picturing all kinds of cute small puppies, yapping and frolicking playfully. She was going to have a hard time choosing just one. Maybe if she begged and pleaded, she would be able to get two puppies. When they were taken back to the kennels, her heart was broken. They only had three dogs, and two growled and snapped at the cages they were in, and the last was a sad-eyed broken mixed Labrador retriever. So by default, they brought home the lab. She decided to make the best of a bad situation, and named the dog Tipsy. But even that was taken from her by her father, who started calling the dog Banjo. Somehow, that stupid name stuck, and from that moment on Norma hated the dog.

Norma's backyard led off into the woods, with a path they could follow to a local lake. Her parents would walk with her in the fall, so she could see how the leaves changed colors. Norma loved those walks and seeing the red and yellow shades the trees took on during that time. In the winter, you could still walk down the path; the snow made it a lot harder, but during the winter, the woods took on a different beauty. The trees would be bare of leaves, and as far as you could see there was nothing but white. It reminded her of that song White Christmas. Her father had taken on the responsibility of taking Banjo for his walks. It became a comic routine to hear her father complain about being stuck with the duty. When Norma or her mother would offer to do it, her father would just wave them off and do it anyway. On one occasion, no one was home, so she had no choice but to walk the dog. She was doing fine until the dog decided to start pulling on the leash and trying to run off. As she struggled with the dog, she had another attack. She let go of the leash and fumbled at her pocket, trying to get her inhaler. Norma was on her back staring at the sky by the time she finally recovered. She followed the path to the lake and found the stupid dog waiting for her. She had no problems bringing the dog home, but it was too late; the dog was going to pay. That night when she told her father what had happened, he felt terrible. He told Norma how whenever he took Banjo out they'd jogged to the lake. He told her not to blame the dog, because it was only doing what they normally did. As her father was explaining all this to Norma, the dog was staring up at her with those stupid sad eyes. If her father wasn't there, she would have kicked Banjo in his pathetic face.

The following week, Norma found herself alone again with Banjo. This time when she took him for a walk, she let the leash go. When Norma made it to the lake, Banjo was happily waiting. Norma sat down beside the dog and began to scratch him behind the ears. Banjo soaked up the welcomed affection. When he lifted his head, Norma slid the knife across his throat. The blade bit deep into fur and flesh, and Banjo immediately began to gasp. The dog's eyes stayed looking sad as it tried to hack up the blood so it could breathe. Norma started to laugh and shake as she watched Banjo die. Norma was sure she'd have an attack but never did. She actually felt great and found herself yelling at Banjo, asking if he liked this feeling. She grabbed the dead dog's mouth and began to fish in her pocket for her inhaler. When she saw all the blood, Norma snapped out of her delirium and started to take control of herself again. She removed the rope she had in her fanny pack. She tied one end to a big rock and the other to Banjo's body. She was able to lift the rock with both hands and toss it into the lake. Norma started to gasp for breath, but she took two quick puffs off her inhaler. She had to remind herself that there was no need to rush. After a few minutes, she dragged Banjo into the lake, and was pleased to see that no one would be able to spot him from the shore. The water removed almost all of the blood from her clothes, but she was still going to throw everything in the wash. Norma walked over and picked up her father's knife. She didn't remember dropping it, and when she saw that it was free of blood, she smiled. All she had to do was return it to her father's study, and he would never know what it was used for. On the walk back from the lake, she was practically skipping. Norma had finally done something without having a n asthma attack. Granted, many would feel what she did was sick and twisted, but those would be the same assholes who teased her. By the time her father came home she had already washed her clothes and showered. She began to cry hysterically as she told the story of Banjo running away. Her father told her to just calm down as she took two puffs off of her inhaler. He promised that once Banjo got hungry he'd return and that she shouldn't worry. It rained that night, and her father sat on the back porch. That was something he never did before, but he made it a vigil from that day until he died. Norma felt terrible about how hurt her father became at the loss of Banjo.As she sat on the bench remembering this, she contemplated scuba-diving for his bones. She'd retrieve Banjo's bones and bury them with her father. Well, that sounded good, but she couldn't scuba-dive because of her asthma. Besides, even if she could and did retrieve his bones, she'd just keep them as a reminder of her first victim. She had read in her detective magazines that serial killers keep mementos of their victims. Norma knew that the magazine was referring to human victims, but it was her first victim and should count for something. When she entered high school, Norma decided to go extreme to be accepted; she was going to become the school tramp. Her problem was never her looks. Truth be told, Norma was very attractive. With her long black hair, blue eyes, and large breasts, a lot of boys gawked at her. If it wasn't for her affliction, she would probably have been highly sought after by the guys. There was this one guy named Jeffrey Wilson who was considered the class rebel. Norma decided that she would make advances towards him, and let him take her virginity. Norma figured that once Jeffrey went around bragging to everyone about what they had done, other guys would come running.

Norma's advances on Jeffrey paid off, and one night, she got him to come over to her house. Her parents had to go out for the evening and wouldn't be home until late. Her and Jeffrey were making out hot and heavy on her bed. When Jeffrey reached down and undid her pants the excitement became too much for her, and she had an asthma attack.

She must have passed out at some point because when she woke up, her pants were off. What was worse was that between her legs was hurting badly, and blood was on her legs and blanket. The jerk had sex with her while she was unconscious, and left her when he was done! The next day at school, Norma expected to have a bunch of guys approach her for dates, but not one did. When she walked the halls, she didn't see anyone pointing and giggling at her. Norma waited a week before she came to the conclusion that Jeffrey didn't tell anyone what they did. He had avoided her all week, but she decided to confront him after school. He'd either start telling people she was easy, or have a dose of poison slipped into his soda at lunch. When Jeffrey saw her on his motorcycle after school, he was not happy. He was even less happy when Norma laid into him about his lack of decency for not telling anyone at school that he'd had sex with her. That's when Jeffrey broke down and split his guts. He had only recently taken on the rebel image so people would think he was cool. Before he changed his image, he was viewed as a geek and no one would talk to him. He would have gladly told people what they'd done, but he was still in shock over it himself. He had only made it as far as second base before and couldn't believe he made it home.

At some point, Jeffrey asked her if she enjoyed it, and Norma had to remind him that she was unconscious. He begged her for forgiveness and asked her to be his girlfriend. Norma was actually intrigued about being Jeffrey's girlfriend; this would secure her social acceptance. He told her to give him her answer later when he came by her house. He kissed her before starting his motorcycle and driving away. When he was about twenty feet from her, he turned his head to look back. In that instant, he shot into an intersection and was creamed by a bus. Norma was still standing in the same spot when the police arrived on the scene. Later that night, Norma sat in her room, stewing about the day. How could she be so stupid to give her virginity to such a moron? She imagined herself as the bus driver. Once she hit Jeffrey the first time, she would have thrown the bus in reverse and ran over his dumb ass again. His death had ruined everything. She couldn't very well tell people they had sex without him alive to verify it. The people at school would only think she was saying it to be noticed. She thought about going back to her original plan of being the school tramp, but she changed her mind quickly. She wasn't too keen on having continual asthma attacks every time she was caught up in the heat of the moment. Norma suffered through high school the same as she did in junior high and elementary. Once she entered college, Norma decided to just be who she was and deal with it. That was until she bought a detective magazine with an article that peaked her interest. The story was about a female student at another college. This student went to the police and told them how one of her professors was forcing sex on her for a good grade. Working with the police, she brought down the professor and became very popular. Norma had to laugh at a side article that said the student later did a naked photo shoot and starred in several pornos. Norma decided that this was a perfect opportunity and even knew the professor that she could blame. He was always making lewd advances at his female students and suggested that they come back after school for extra tutoring. Norma spent the remainder of the night thinking of a convincing story to tell the Dean the next day. She figured once that she started talking and getting all emotional she'd most likely have an asthma attack. No one likes to see a person with a disability taken advantage of; that in itself would help cook the professor's goose. The next morning as she approached the Dean's building, she noticed two police cars parked in front. She approached a small crowd that had gathered to discover what was happening. One of the people told her that a female student had come forward and accused a professor of forcing sex for good grades. Norma could only stare at the Dean's building in disbelief.

Now, two years removed from College, Norma sat on the park bench, contemplating this newest failure. She considered maybe forgoing human victims and killing pets. She had one pet already in the books, and she was pretty sure she never heard of a pet serial killer. As she was thinking this, her imagination took hold of her. Norma found herself attending a meeting of Serial Killers Anonymous. At this meeting when she stood up and said that she was a newly reformed pet serial killer, the crowd burst into tears laughing. That snapped Norma out of her daydream and back to the present.Norma took a few more moments to gather herself then rose from the bench. She noticed another elderly woman in a pink jogging suit passing by. Norma was about to head back home when she suddenly stopped to take a close look at the woman. She wasn't jogging, she was walking. A big smile formed on Norma's face as she remembered hearing about people doing something called " power walking." OH, THE SWEET SMELL OF SUCCESS, Norma thought as she rubbed her thumb along the steak knife and headed down the trail after the elderly woman.

THE WHEEZER 2: THIS PUFFS FOR YOU!

Norma stared in the mirror and gently touched the bruise underneath her eye. It had been almost a week since the attack, and the bruise only just recently begun to fade.

Who would've known that the power-walking elderly woman also had aspirations to be a serial killer. It seemed at the time that she was finally going to make her first kill. Then, as she got closer the elderly lady turned and punched in the face causing her to fall to the ground. Unfortunately, it also caused Norma to drop the steak knife she was holding. Which the elderly lady quickly picked up and would have used on Norma had two men jogging not came upon the scene and made a citizen's arrest.

The televisions and newspapers ate the whole situation up, dubbing the elderly lady, "The Senior Slasher." To make matters worse Norma's name was only mentioned briefly as the victim and witness for the state when it finally made it to trial. Norma was supposed to be the one who's life was being run through a microscope, not the stupid elderly lady. This was supposed to be her moment in the spotlight. She was the one who was going to be led into the courtroom and become a legend. The lady's story wasn't even a good one. The lady claimed that she decided to turn to a life of crime due to society. No one would give her a decent paying job at her age. Her son and daughter were working on putting her in a nursing home. Her social security check wasn't enough to pay for anything these days. So she decided to go out and become a serial killer with the intention of being caught. This way she could go to prison and get free room and board. Not have to worry where her next meal was coming from and receive free dental and medical. The more Norma thought about it the more she realized the lady's story was actually a good one. Maybe that was why a lot of people were sympathetic to the lady, and were even picketing the courthouse on her behalf. One group that wasn't on the elderly lady's side were the animal activists. It made headlines that what drove the lady over the edge was her pet Conver. The bird wouldn't stop squawking, which with everything else that was going on in her life caused her to snap. So on the morning of the attack, before she left the house she took the bird out of his cage, tossed him in her microwave and pressed the chicken button. The police, when contacted about the incident, would not confirm or deny the details. They would only say that Carlton the Conver did indeed have a tragic accident on the morning in question.

Norma walked out of the bathroom and sat on her sofa, trying to think of what to do next. It was obvious that serial killer was now totally out of the question. If she did anything like that now she'd be only seen as a copycat. Not to mention they'd say she did it due to the trauma she received at the hands of the elderly lady. Which would only add to the popularity of the so-called, "Senior Slasher."

Norma began to wonder if she might be going about this all wrong. Maybe what he needed to be successful was a partner. The problem was the only person she could think of who hated people as much as Norma was a blonde girl who worked in her office named Renee. Renee had to wear these really thick glasses because her eyesight was so bad. She had told Norma how all her life people made fun of her, and she'd love someday to pay them back. In this way she was a kindred spirit with Norma. They could use their anger as a motivating reason to go on a nation-wide crime spree. The media would probably call them the real-life versions of Thelma and Louise.

Norma took a puff from her inhaler as the excitement of the possibility brought her to the brink of an asthma attack. As the medicine began to take effect and her head began to clear, she realized the ideas were flawed. It was true that Renee and her were equals in some things, but intelligence wasn't one of them. Truth be told, Renee was as dumb as a box of rocks. Rumor had it that the only reason she kept her job was because she did favors for the boss. So, in the end it wouldn't be like Thelma and Louise. It would end up more like that Blonde and Brunette bank robber joke; the Brunette tells the Blonde to go into the bank and tie up the guard and blow open the safe while the Brunette waits for her in the getaway car. After the Blonde enters the bank a few minutes go bye, then the bank alarm sounds. The Blonde comes out of the bank trying to drag the safe by a rope as the guard chases after her while trying to pull up his pants.

Norma giggled as she pictured the whole scenario playing out in her head. They would definitely end up getting caught and become co-defendants. The problem with that is there's no such thing as a co-defendant. It's more like a defendant and a turn coat. Which would definitely be Renee, who would crack under the State Attorney's pressure. Granted Norma would become famous. However, it would be due to Renee's betrayal. Norma would never be able to let that go, and would go crazy in prison being unable to seek vengeance on Renee for her betrayal. So after those thoughts, Norma dismissed the idea of seeking a partner in crime. Norma grabbed a pen and paper off the coffee table and made a note that if she changed her mind about becoming a serial killer to make her first victim Renee... that treacherous back-stabbing tramp.

Norma put the pen and paper back on the table and picked up the latest crime magazine. After glancing through it for a few minutes she came across an article about a crazed survivalist who was killed by the FBI at his secluded compound. Now here's something that might have potential. It shouldn't be too hard to find one of these survivalist groups and sign up. Once a member, they could teach her how to use different kinds of weapons and survive in the wilderness. The longer she pondered this idea the more she realized these groups do a lot of physical training. With her asthma she'd never be able to do all that strenuous exercising. Besides, they have no sense of style. All they wear is camouflage outfits. Not to mention they crawl on the ground with all those creepy crawly things. Norma shivered at that thought. Well that's a definite not-going-to-happen Norma decided.

Norma placed the magazine on the table and leaned back into the cushions. Why was it so difficult to come up with an idea to do something to become famous? The survivalist group had some potential, but she needed something less physical. She sat up straight and smiled as the image popped in her head of a biker gang. She could go to one of those biker bars and become a biker babe. She'd look good in tight leather, and she'd have the best of both worlds. The biker gang could teach her how to use weapons, and she could talk them into going on a nation-wide crime spree. As she thought about the motorcycle her mind flashed back to that moron ex-boyfriend she had in highschool. The thought of a bus coming out of nowhere and flattening him caused her to start reconsidering this idea. Besides, with her asthma, would she even be able to breath on a motorcycle as it sped down the highway? Then there's the sex; most bikers are fat, out of shape slobs. Granted many aren't, but with her luck she could see how this would end up. She'd get some beer but the loser would get on top of her and she'd have an attack due to being smothered by the idiot. No Norma thought to herself as she leaned back again this idea was no good for us either.

With a sigh of frustration, she rose from the couch and decided to go for a walk around the neighborhood. Maybe the fresh air of the night would bring her fresh ideas. As she exited her apartment and headed down the street a semi truck roared bye. Norma stared at the truck's tail lights as it stopped at a red light. The thought of maybe becoming a rest stop serial killer popped into her mind and then quickly popped out again. She didn't see herself hitching rides in semis across the country. Rest stops were far from clean, and she'd probably end up hitching a ride with a psychotic truck driver and end up a statistic. She decided to keep the idea on the back burner and maybe work out the kinks keeping it as a last resort. What she could do is fall back on the old faithful. She could once again become a pet serial killer. She'd go to the pet store and buy a goldfish. For the first few days she'd feed it, then just stop. She'd watch the goldfish swim around in a panic. Then, after a few days she'd sprinkle sand into the water instead of food. She could picture the poor goldfish sucking in the particles of sand and spitting it back out once it realized it wasn't food. Norma laughed as she imagined the fish thinking to herself, "WHY HAVE YOU FORSAKEN ME, GOD OF THE YUMMY FLAKES!"

Norma watched as an elderly lady who was walking towards her quickly crossed the street. Norma realized how she might look to other people, just walking and laughing to herself. Then her facial expression changed to one of anger as she couldn't even kill pets. That stupid elderly lady nuked her Conver. Even if she tried to be a pet serial killer she'd again only be considered a copycat. Sure she could always bring them to Banjo's watery grave, but he'd only be bones by now. So that really wouldn't prove her case. Then what if the police did raid her house. Would a goldfish lying belly up in a fishbowl be considered a murder scene? She highly doubted it.

To Norma's surprise she had already circumvented her block and was approaching her apartment. As she began to climb the steps of her building, the ultimate idea dawned on her. She could achieve everything she had ever wanted and do it legally. She could cause pain and heartache throughout society and be remembered in history. She could even announce her intentions to the public after the elderly lady's trial. She might not be the headliner of the trial, but the media would definitely want an interview with her once the trial ended and every day after it.

¤ ¤ ¤

The two officers led the elderly lady back to her cell block. The trial had lasted about two weeks and today they found her guilty. However, despite the State Attorney's best efforts all they could convict her on was Aggravated Battery with a weapon. Which she hoped the judge would sentence her to the maximum that charge carried at her sentencing date next week. She doubted at her age she'd live to see the release date, but she couldn't be sure. Prison was awful, but she'd get three meals a day, her laundry done, free dental and medical, and a bed to sleep in. This was guaranteed to her by the state as a prisoner. Where if she was free there was no guarantee she'd receive anything. That was the main reason for all this, no benefits to help a person of her age by the government.

As she entered the cell block she saw her friend on the television. She walked closer and heard the reporter ask what Norma was going to add to now that the trial was over. With a big smile Norma turned to the camera and said she was going to run for a political office in the next election. The elderly lady turned from the television and thought to herself, "Well played Wheezer, well played.

THE LEGEND OF EGG ROCK

The wound was severe, but she was still able to carry her egg across the ocean to this spot. She laid it in the water and settled on a nearby cluster of rocks. The blood flowed from the gash in her side, down her ebony black scales and drenched the rocks below her. Her massive wings flapped spasmodically, despite her effort to ignore the pain. The wind created by her wings caused the ocean to toss and turn as if a typhoon had hit the area. The dragon bared her teeth at the thought of the human knight who snuck into her lair and attacked her while she slept. A sorcerer, she thought to herself. A sorcerer had to have assisted him in entering her domain without alarming her to his presence. The knight was too anxious to make the kill and struck wildly. Had he been patient he would have succeeded. Instead, she was able to grab her egg and flee. They would all pay for this insolence after she rested and healed, no matter how long it takes.

Her eyes squinted as she focused on the water near her egg. A creature, no, creatures, were moving through the water towards her. One had made the costly mistake of breaking away from the main group and moving towards her egg. She may have been injured, but her head flashed forward in a blink of an eye and snatched the creature out of the water before it could reach its destination. With a flip of her head, the creature was swallowed. She knew what sort of creatures she was dealing with: sea ghouls. The creatures were once sailors who in life ate human flesh. When they died this unnatural hunger brought them back in the form of these abominations. The surface of the water broke in front of the blood red rocks. A lone creature moved out of the water and knelt before the massive dragon. She stared at this creature with its head bowed before her, Its long stringy hair plastered to its scalp, long arms propped on a bent knee with razor sharp claws glistening in the sun. The flesh on its body seemed to hang onto its bones as if it was mere decoration.

"We come in peace. O Scourge of the Skies,' the ghoul hissed without raising its head. 'Your wings caused the oceans to roll as if a storm hit. When the oceans act like this, ships are bound to crash. My people and I merely came to feast on any fool caught in such a storm.

Her head began to lower and her eyes closed from the loss of blood. She shook her head to rid herself of the sleepy feeling, and peered down at the blood covered rocks. The ghoul must have been able to sense how hurt she was. But even in this condition, she was way more than a match against these wretches.

'A mistake, O Mightiest of Horrors,' the ghoul moaned. 'My people have always been friends of dragons. It was my people who killed and ate the crew of The Avenger. That was the ship that killed the sea dragon Bedimir.

'When your people finished with the crew didn't they return and eat Bedimir?' She asked, tapping one of her talons on the rock angrily.

'It was a service my lady!' The ghoul wailed. 'We only did that to honor Bedimir! Had we not done so, his body would have laid at the bottom of the ocean rotting. That would surely have been a dishonorable end to such a legendary dragon.'

'Bedimirs fate is truly none of my concern,' she replied. 'However, you and your people will do me a service for the attack on my egg.'

'Yes, O Queen of Death. It will be our honor,' the ghoul said as it flattened itself onto the rocks as if in worship.

'The rocks that we stand on are infused with my blood. They will remain red from this day forward, as long as blood is spilt on them.

When you and your people feed, do it here from this day forth. As long as the rocks remain red, I will be drawn back to this location,' the dragon ordered, flexing its wings and trying to ease the pain in her side. "That is only part of the service you and your people will do. the other part that you'll do will be to protect my egg until I return.'

'But what if it hatches before your return?' The ghoul asked, still sprawled before the dragon.

'It won't,' the dragon replied, then spoke a few words in the dragon language. As the last words were spoken, she pointed at the egg, and it turned into a large rock."

"So what happened to the dragon?" The small blonde haired girl asked, looking up at her grandfather. "Did it die?"

"You know, you really are impatient," her grandfather said with a smile as he squeezed her hand gently. "Okay, where was I?" Oh yeah..."

"Once the egg was turned into a rock, she flapped her wings and rose into the sky.

The ghoul rose and watched as the dragon flew north. As he looked out into the ocean at the egg, he shook his head. He knew that dragons were hard to hurt. But once they were it took forever for them to heal. He could sense how bad the dragon's wound was. In truth, he and his people came here in hopes of a dragon flesh feast, they remembered the taste of Bedimir, and how the magic in the dragon's blood made them much stronger. Unfortunately, instead of a meal, they were now bound to protect her egg until her return. That wound would take hundreds of years to heal if it healed at all. There was no telling when or if she'd ever return!

A drop of rain splashed on the grandfather's nose as he finished his story. He looked up and saw how dark the sky was and realized they had to get home. As he knelt down to button his granddaughter's jacket, he noticed a strange man. He had salt and pepper hair and wore a black trench coat. He was standing a few feet away and staring out at Egg Rock.

"Well, come on, let's get you home." he said, picking his granddaughter up in his arms. "We don't want to be caught up in the rain now, do we?"

"AAA, AAH, no rain," the little girl laughed. "I can't wait to get home and tell Mommy the story you told me."

"Oh, great," he replied smiling. "So, if you have nightmares, guess who's a dead man?"

"Don't be silly. Grandpa. I'm not going to have nightmares,' she laughed. "I'm a big girl!"

"Yes, you are," he said, hugging her close to him as they headed to their car.

"So what's going to happen when the dragon finally comes back for her egg?" The little girl asked, looking around her grandfather's shoulder back at Egg Rock.

"Well, Lynn, Swampscott, and a few other Massachusetts cities are in some big trouble," her grandfather replied, "No one's prepared for anything like that.'

"You'd be surprised." the man in the trench coat said to himself softly, smiling as he patted the magic sword concealed beneath his coat.

MELISSA

"This happened just before the Salem Witch trials" Jasper said with the hint of a smile.

"Carl did not want to believe Jasper's stories."

He was sure that he was only trying to spook him with his ghost stories.

"You're just making this up," he said. "You're just trying to scare me!"

"No, I'm not. It's true. I swear!" Jasper replied as he moved the lock of white hair from his eyes.

Carl had just moved with his parents from Tempe, Arizona to Lynn, Massachusetts. He had always been able to make friends quickly, and after they had settled in, he met Jasper. At first, Carl didn't know what to make of Jasper. He always dressed in black which matched the color of his hair except one lock of white hair which he constantly played with. He was tall for being only fourteen and pale-skinned. Jasper lived with a foster family by the name of Menard. Whenever Carl would go over and visit, he couldn't help but feel uncomfortable.

Jasper's foster parents, the Menards, were the opposite of Jasper. Mr. and Mrs. Menard were both short of build with graying, blond hair. The Menards seemed to be nice, but to Carl it seemed to be more of an act than real. Jasper's presence around his foster parents seemed to make them timid. To Carl, it seemed to him like the way animals reacted around a predator. If it wasn't for all the cool stuff Jasper had in his room, Carl doubted he'd continue going over to visit. Jasper's room was decorated with posters of famous horror movies. His shelves had finished models of movie monsters in different scary poses. The coolest things were the video games: Wolfsbane 1 and 2, Build Me A Monster, and Zombie Inc.

"So let me see if I heard you correctly," Carl said as he and Jasper walked down the sidewalk on Boston Street. " There were two sisters, Abigail and Melissa."

"Identical twin sisters," Jasper interrupted.

"Oh, right, so these sisters were witches, and they lived in Salem. Now one of the sisters had to go to Boston to go shopping."

"Well, actually, Melissa had to go and pick up some special plants sold at a shop in Boston," Jasper said with a smile.

"Okay. So Melissa leaves her sister Abigail in Salem. And both sisters were very beautiful, tall with high cheekbones, and long black hair."

"With a lock of white in their hair," Jasper said, holding his own lock out towards Carl.

"Yeah, right. Anyway, while Melissa's away, a priest named Johnson sees Abigail dancing naked by the light of the moon three nights before 'All Hallow's Eve' and informs the town council. The townspeople storm Abigail and Melissa's house and drag Abigail, kicking and screaming, to a giant rock. Now, Abigail was tied ' spread eagle' under a rock that was lifted by ropes, and the townspeople started lowering the rock onto her.

While this was going on, Father Johnson was reading verses from the Bible and telling Abigail to confess her sins and repent. As the rock began to crush her, she screamed and cursed, and then with her last breath,she screamed her sister's name and died."

"While this was happening, Melissa had returned from Boston only to find the house ransacked. She followed the screaming and hollering and watched, while hidden in the woods, as the townspeople killed Abigail. That night deep in the woods, Melissa called upon her dark lord to assist her in her desire to seek vengeance upon the townspeople. She gave herself to him and took his seed. A strong urge overtook her, and she began to crave the blood of the innocent. Not only innocent, but uncorrupted, the blood of children."

"On the night of 'All Hallow's Eve' at twelve midnight, the 'Witching Hour,' Melissa entered the town of Salem and began taking children out of their bedroom windows and feeding on their blood."

"In the morning, the town was filled with the wailing of parents who found the torn and bloodless bodies of their children outside their bedroom windows. A lynch mob was quickly formed, and despite a thorough search of the woods, there was no sign of Melissa to be found anywhere."

"Nine months passed with no sign of Melissa, until one night when the air was filled with the sounds of a woman screaming. The townspeople followed the sound to an open glade where Melissa laid on the ground in the process of giving birth. Father Johnson began reciting verses out of the Bible as the townspeople tried to kill Melissa, but no matter how hard they tried, no weapon could touch Melissa or her newborn baby boy."

"He won't let you harm us,' Melissa hissed."

"The baby and Melissa were taken back to the town of Salem and placed under heavy guard. Despite numerous attempts to figure out a way for the town to be rid of this evil, nothing seemed to work."

"On a dark and stormy night three days before the following 'All Hallow's Eve,' a dark-cloaked figure entered a meeting in the town hall to the shock of the townspeople. When the hood of the cloak was lowered, the face of a beautiful blond-haired woman was revealed. She introduced herself as Meredith Smith, and she knew how to deal with Melissa. However, a pact has to be made between the church and her coven."

"The townspeople, who normally would have dragged Meredith to the crushing rock, were begging Father Johnson to agree. Father Johnson reluctantly consented, and Meredith told him what had to be done."

"In a nearby township named Lynn a small church was located in a graveyard, or in other terms, 'hallowed ground.' On 'All Hallow's Eve' at the the stroke of midnight, the 'Witching Hour,' Father Johnson and Meredith had to place Melissa and the baby in the church. Then with their combined effort, bind her there for all eternity.

Now, on 'All Hallow's Eve,' anyone who has not entered adulthood and has the blood of the innocent, and is foolish enough to be caught in that church during the 'Witching Hour,' is prey for Melissa." Carl shook his head when he was finished with the retelling of Jasper's story. He looked at the white lock of hair on Jasper and wanted to laugh at him for giving the character of his story the same trait.

"We're here!" Jasper said as he stopped so suddenly that Carl walked past him and stumbled to a stop.

Carl looked at a large, brown-stoned church with large picture windows. A large set of stone steps led up to two dark brown, wooden doors. The building itself was surrounded by a metal fence with pointed tips on the top of each pole.

"You wanted to visit a church?" Carl asked with a confused look on his face.

"This is Sacred Heart Church," Jasper said, holding up his hands at the building as if to emphasize the point. "I have a friend named Father Johanson I want you to meet. And he can verify my story."

The two boys walked around the side of the church and knocked on a wooden door with a glass window. After a few minutes, an older man with gray touching the sides of his dark brown hair opened the door. He was dressed in the typical all black of the church with a white collar.

"Jasper, what are you doing here?" The man asked with a look of shock on his face. "Is everything okay?" Are you and your friend here in some kind of trouble?"

"Oh, no, Father Johanson, nothing like that," Jasper said with a smile. "I just wanted you to meet my new friend Carl and answer some questions for him."

"Sure, sure, come on in. I'm sure I can find a few minutes to spare for you two boys," he said with a smile as he ushered them inside.

They walked down a hall and entered an office with a large desk and two light brown chairs facing it. The walls were lined with bookshelves, and behind the desk was a large picture window. Once everyone was seated, Father Johanson placed his elbows on the desk and placed his hands together in a steeple position as he stared at the two boys. "So, how can I help you?"

"He wants to know about Melissa," Jasper replied with a grin on his face.

Father Johanson leaned back in his chair as if he'd been slapped and made a sucking sound with his teeth. "I don't think this is the time or the place for such a story, do you, Jasper?"

"Well, actually, I do since this is Halloween and I already told him most of it." Jasper's grin widened.

"Jasper says the story's true, but I have to admit I don't believe him," Carl said, trying not to look at Father Johanson and tapping his hand nervously on the arm rest of the chair.

"It's human nature to question anything we hear. Especially a story like the one Jasper told you," Father Johanson said reassuringly. "However, most stories like that originate from some form of truth."

"So the stories are true?" Carl said as his eyes almost bulged out of his head, and he looked as if he wanted to bolt out of the room.

"See, I told you so!" Jasper said, leaning back in his chair triumphantly.

"Hold on now, I didn't say that," Father Johanson said, lifting his hand as if issuing a stop sign. "All I'm saying is during that time period, a lot of bad things happened and due to some tragic event, the story of

Melissa and Abigail originated. I think that people changed the story over the years into a 'ghost story' to keep kids from playing in Pine Grove Cemetery on Halloween night."

"Well, we'll find out tonight if it's true or not," Jasper replied with a smile from ear to ear.

"We will?" Carl said with a terrified look on his face.

"Unless, of course, you're chicken," Jasper said, placing his fists on his sides to make his arms look like wings and waving them up and down as if flapping like a bird.

"I'm not chicken," Carl said angrily. "I'm not afraid of some stupid ghost story!"

"Then it's settled. At twelve o'clock tonight, you and I will go to that little church and see if Melissa's real or not, " Jasper said, looking at Carl as if what he said was some kind of challenge.

"Wait, wait, wait!" Father Johanson said, wagging his finger at the boys.

"The cemetery is not a playground, and besides, there are laws against trespassing. I highly recommend you two put such foolish notions behind you..."

"Whatever you say, Father Johanson," Jasper said as he cut off Father Johanson and stood from his chair. "Carl and I are going to the library and talk to Miss Melanie. Thanks for taking the time to see us."

"Oh, it was my pleasure, boys, anytime," Father Johanson said as he rose from behind the desk and escorted the boys to the exit.

"Remember what I said boys," Father said again as he waved good-bye. "The cemetery is no place to be playing at night."

Carl climbed the marble stairs leading to the front doors of the library. When he first saw the Lynn Public Library, he couldn't help but think hoe ouy of place it looked. The building was made in an old Roman style fashion, with large pillars on each side of the front doors.

It was a well-done re-creation of buildings of that time period. Then, when you looked next door, you saw the red-bricked Boys Club building and couldn't help but laugh at the irony.

"Lynn, Lynn, the city of sin,
You never come out, the way you went in."

Jasper was singing as he opened the door and entered the library.

"What's that you're going on about?" Carl asked as he followed Jasper through the doors and into the library.

"It's an old poem about the city," Jasper replied in a soft voice.

"Doesn't make you feel good about living here, does it?" Carl whispered back.

"Lynn is the city where evil things dwell. They come here to live to be closer to hell," Jasper said with a grin.

"Jasper," a woman's voice said from behind the desk.

As the boys looked in the direction of the information desk, a talk woman with short blond hair in a gray business suit walked from around the desk and towards them. Carl guessed the woman to be in her forties, but she was very pretty for her age.

"Hi, Miss Melanie. Me and my friend, Carl, came to see you," Jasper said happily.

"Well, that was nice of you. Are you here to check out some books?" Miss Melanie asked.

"We were hoping we could talk to you for a moment about Melissa," Jasper said softly. "I was telling Carl the story, but he doesn't believe me, you can tell."

"I never said I didn't believe you. I just said it's a made-up ghost story to scare people, that's all," Carl replied defensively. "Even Father Johanson said pretty much the same thing."

"Well, why don't you two follow me to my office," Miss Melanie said. "This way. I might be able to shed some light on the legend, and we won't disturb the people while they're reading."

Carl and Jasper followed Miss Melanie to her office, and once they were seated, Carl repeated the story as he heard it before. The office reminded Carl of Father Johanson's in the way it was set up. A desk, two chairs, bookshelves, and a picture window, but where the chairs in Father Johanson's were comfortable to sit in, these were hard and squeaked when moved.

"For the most part you have the Legend of Melissa correct, but you don't mention the blood moon," Miss Melanie said looking at Jasper questioningly. "It's a part of the three-fold law that was used to bind Melissa to the church at Pine Grove Cemetery. On 'All Hallow's Eve', at the 'Witching Hour', under a blood-red moon, Melissa was entombed. So the legend goes, and only when these three things occur, can she awaken and roam her tomb hoping to feed on the blood of the innocent."

"That's the part I always forget," Jasper smiled.

"Whatever happened to the baby?" Carl asked. "I mean, there's no mention of him."

"You're correct about thar Carl," Miss Melanie replied as she leaned forward in her chair. "All the stories written about Melissa exclude what happened to the baby."

"And why is that?" Jasper asked, leaning forward and looking at Miss Melanie expectantly.

"Well, maybe, it was never disclosed what actually happened to the baby that night, or despite who the baby's parents were, it was innocent and had no real bearing on the story," Miss Melanie said leaning back with a smile.

"Thanks for seeing us, Miss Melanie," Jasper said as he got up from the chair. "It's about time Carl and I got going. We have a big night ahead of us."

"Oh, are you boys going trick-or-treating?" Miss Melanie asked with a smile as she rose to show them out.

"Nah, Carl and I are going to the cemetery to see if the story of Melissa is true," Jasper said as Carl and him headed out the door.

"Just hold on a minute, boys," Miss Melanie said as she placed a hand on each of their shoulders. "There are laws against trespassing in a cemetery after dark. Not to mention it is the resting place for the deceased. I hope you two put any such notions out of your heads and find another way to enjoy your Halloween."

¤ ¤ ¤

It was around eleven-thirty when Carl snuck out of his bedroom window and met Jasper on Boston Street. As they walked, Carl stared at the stone wall they neared. It was up to Carl's head, and he could easily pull himself up onto it if he wanted to. A crop of the wall into darkness.

"Did you know this is the second largest man-made stone wall in the world," Jasper said, skimming his hand along it as they walked."

"No, it's not," Carl replied. "You're just making that up."

"No, no, really! When they tore down the Berlin Wall, this officially took over second place to the Great Wall of China," Jasper replied, shaking his head up and down as if to verify his own point.

"Where'd you hear that from? Carl asked, looking at his friend as if he was totally gullible.

"Actually, a whole bunch of people have told me that," Jasper said defensively.

"Well, it goes to show you that a whole bunch of people are idiots," Carl said which caused both the boys to laugh. As fast as the laughter started, it stopped once they turned the corner of the wall and saw the entrance to Pine Grove Cemetery.

"Look," Jasper said pointing up into the sky. "The moon's full, and it's red."

"Maybe we should listen to the warnings about trespassing in a cemetery at night. Like they said, it's illegal," Carl said trying to hide the quiver in his voice. "We don't want to get into any trouble."

"Oh my god, you're scared!" Jasper said looking at Carl with a big smile on his face. "It's only a coincidence, Carl, nothing to be afraid of."

"I'm not afraid," Carl said as he walked through the gate and into the cemetery.Once inside, both boys couldn't help but notice how the breeze wasn't blowing as hard as before. They entered, and even though they were next to a busy street, it wasn't noisy as it should be. A small blue house was on the right as they entered, and a short distance down the road stood the small church.

"Does anyone live in this house?" Carl asked as they walked by. "I don't see any lights on."

"It's the cemetery office during the day," Jasper replied as his eyes scanned the trees they passed on the left. "No one lives there now, but a while back a night watchman used to live there. Supposedly, he used to walk the cemetery at night with a shotgun, looking for trespassers. The gun was loaded with rock salt, and if he shot you it would burn like hell, but that's just a story."

"Oh, so that's just some dumb story, but Mellisa's not," Carl said as they approached the steps of the church.

"Pretty much," Jasper said, shrugging his shoulders and pushing the church door open.

"The church had pews on the left and right. At the front of the church was an altar and behind it a large cross. The windows were made with different scenes of the life and death of Jesus. Candles lit the interior and kneeling in the front was a figure covered in a dark cloak.

"Is that Melissa?" Jasper whispered as he nudged Carl.

"How the hell should I know?" Carl said angrily. "This waz your stupid idea, why don't you go ask?"

"That won't be necessary," a male voice said from behind them.

When the boys turned, they were shocked to see the Menards standing in front of the door.

"I don't understand," Jasper said, looking at them confused. "What are you doing here?"

"Welcome, Father Johnson and Lady Meredith," the cloaked figure said as it stood, removing the hood and turning to reveal the face of Melissa. "How nice of you to come visit. I'd offer you something to eat, but I don't think there's enough to go around."

"You can't have him, Melissa," Lady Meredith said, moving forward and putting a hand on Jasper's shoulder. "We've adopted him. He's our son."

"Oh, now therein lies the problem," Melissa said with a mocking smile. "By the rules he's now mine, and since they're your rules, well, it sucks to be you!"

"Come on Merry," Father Johnson said, draping his arm around her and leading her back out the door. "She's right, he came here on his own free will."

"Mom, Dad, please don't leave!" Jasper yelled with tears in his eyes, but when he made it to the door, it was already closed and locked. "Come on, Carl, help me get this door open so we can get out of here!"

"I'm sorry, Jasper, I just can't do that, Carl said as he moved over to stand next to Melissa. "My Mom wouldn't like it"

"Your Mom?" Jasper began to say in disbelief until he actually looked at Carl and Melissa standing next to each other and could see the resemblance. "But... ," Jasper started to say something, but Carl interrupted.

"But the hair's different, right?" Carl said, running his fingers through his blonde hair. "I dyed it, just like you did to get that white lock you have like my Mother's. Oh, and if you're wondering why I look your age? It's my curse, the one you were wondering about, the one that's not told. I will always look like the innocent on which I now feed upon."

"We're friends!" Jasper sobbed as he looked at Carl pleadingly!

"Oh, my sweet Carl," Melissa said, raising her lip to reveal razor-sharp teeth, "How many times must I tell you? NEVER PLAY WITH YOUR FOOD!"

HARM YE NONE

He stared from behind the police crime scene tape and held back a smile as they made the outline of the body. He enjoyed committing the murders, but he absolutely loved watching them trace his bloody creations.

The media had named him the Black Rose Killer, due to him leaving a single black rose at each murder sight.

The police had their own theories on why he left the roses, but their theories were all wrong.He simply left the roses as a thank you to these beautiful women for their participation in the creation of his masterpieces.

Once the police officer finished tracing the outline of his latest creation, he turned and walked away. He only lived five blocks away from the newest addition to his art gallery and wanted to enjoy the night air.

As he walked he couldn't help but laugh at the stupidity of the police. They know that most serial killers stay and watch from the crowd at a murder scene. The thing is how often do you see on the news, " Killer Caught While Watching At Scene." You don't and you never will.

The police don't want to solve a crime the obvious way. They want high tech solutions, DNA, forensics, mass man hunts, and bringing the local criminal offenders in for questioning as potential suspects. It's how they are able to justify their request to the government for more money to fight crime.

He should be sitting in a prison cell right now waiting for his turn to ride the needle. All it would have taken was just one police officer to have actually looked at him. Most of the time they just don't want to be bothered. They are too focused on how they are not a part of the action. They must feel that hanging the crime scene tape and telling onlookers to step back is a waste of their training.

However, if at least one of those officers noticed that this particular onlooker wasn't just bald headed, but also had no eyebrows. They might have become suspicious and ended it all.

He entered his house and headed straight upstairs to put away his newest memento. The girl he had just added to his art gallery had been writing in a book when he crept up behind her and asked if her throat. The book had a weird five pointed star on the cover. Unfortunately, two of the pages now had her blood on them, but he wasn't concerned. Besides it was something of hers that was personal, so he took it for his growing collection.

This last creation was by far his best work yet. He had taken the time to shave off every hair on his body. Then he went to the girl's house and on the side of her building stripped totally naked. He removed the plastic gloves and galoshes from the bag and put them on. Just the thought of what he was about to create gave him an erection, so he covered it with the condom he had brought.

 He could not believe his luck when he found the back door was unlocked. He quietly opened and closed the door. Then cautiously proceeded up the back stairs, looking in rooms he passed until he finally found her. She must have just got out of the shower, because all she was wearing was a towel wrapped around her and her long black hair was still wet looking.

She was so concentrated in what she was writing that she never even heard him creep up behind her. He grabbed and jerked her head back with her long wet hair. Then quickly made a perfect slice across her throat with his knife. She fell back onto the bed grasping at the wound as it poured blood. He slowly positioned himself in front of her, ripped off the towel and entered her.

She never once removed her hands from her damaged throat to fight him off. As he thrusted her blood splashed all over him. He couldn't help but admire her determination to prolong what little life she still had left. He stared into her light blue eyes, remembering that the eyes were the doorway to the soul, but her eyes only seemed to register acceptance as her soul passed from this earth.

Once it was over he walked into her bathroom, flushed the condom, and showered off the blood. When he had finished he wrapped the book in a fresh towel and dropped it out of the bedroom window. He knew that he wouldn't be able to watch the police outline his newest creation if he left her in the house, so he grabbed her by the legs and dragged her through the house and outside to the street.

He ran around to the side of the house where he had left his clothes, removed the gloves and galoshes and placed them back in the bag. Then he proceeded to get dressed. As soon as he was finished putting on his clothes, he removed a bottle of lighter fluid from his jacket pocket and saturated the bag and its contents then set it on fire. After this was done he retrieved the book and headed to the nearest pay phone two blocks away to report the murder. He waited about ten minutes after he saw the first police car drive bye before he decided to go back and watch.

He was snapped back to the present by a loud thump from downstairs.

He had no idea what it could be. He lived alone and never in his life owned a pet. He placed the book on the dresser and drew his knife. He slowly moved across the room and through the bedroom door into the hallway.

He began to ease his way down the stairs.

The lights in the house had been turned on prior to his going out earlier, so if indeed this was an intruder they wouldn't be hard to find.

"Thump!"

92

"Thump!"

The noise seemed to be coming from the kitchen. He hated to admit it, but He found himself a little frightened.

Whoever had entered his house was obviously not police, because if they were they would have identified themselves as such and would have already tried to arrest him. So in all likelihood it was probably a burglar. He smiled at the thought of this, the poor fool picked the wrong house to rob. The stupid bastard would never make this mistake again, because in a few minutes he would be dead. He was going to be doing society another great service, besides sharing his artwork, he'd be ridding them of this miscreant.

He moved to the side of the kitchen door and peeked in. There didn't appear to be anyone in sight, so he entered. The kitchen was rather small with only a table, two chairs, and a refrigerator. He walked over to the pantry door with his knife at the ready and swung the door open - empty. He turned and looked across the room to the cellar door suspiciously. He eased his way over to it, slid the lock closed, and shoved one of the chairs under the door knob. He'd seen one to many movies where a person made the mistake of investigating the cellar and paid for it with their lives.

"Thump!"

"Thump!"

The noise was now coming from upstairs. He walked from the kitchen back towards the stairs in total disbelief. There was positively no way anyone could have snuck by him and gone upstairs. The only possible way would be if they went out the back door and reentered through the front, but he would have heard the doors open and close.

He ran back up the stairs taking them two at a time to the top. The hallway was empty, so he looked into the bathroom on the right of the stairs and saw nothing. As he slowly worked his way down the hall he checked the guest room and computer room, but the results were the same - nothing.

As he made his way back into his own room and closed the door he let out a sigh of relief. He was letting paranoia get the best of him. The thumping sound was probably caused by a rat or a squirrel who got into the house somehow. In which case first thing tomorrow morning he'd call an exterminator and let them handle it.

"Thump!"

"Thump!"

He felt his heart begin to pound in his chest as his eyes focused on the bedroom door. Now that the sound was coming from only a few feet away it was too big to be a rat or a squirrel. The door knob began to rattle uncontrollably, as if it was being struck, instead of someone trying to turn and open it.

He had just about enough of this shit! No one was going to get away with doing this to him. He reached over and yanked the door open. The sight before him caused him to let out a blood curtailing scream.

There standing before him was a police outline, its body was nothing but a twirling mist and the head was the ghostly face of his latest creation.

¤ ¤ ¤

The following morning....

As the two police officers ascended the stairs, they readied their weapons. The hysterical laughter emanating from this house had been the cause of numerous phone calls to the station throughout the night.

A quick search of the downstairs revealed nothing. The only thing that struck them as odd was a chair pushed under The doorknob leading to the basement. Which once it was removed and the door opened proved to be empty.

Once they had reached the top of the stairs they yelled out, identifying themselves as police officers. They had done the same when they first entered the house, but just like earlier the only response was the laughter.

The door to the room from which the laughter was originating was open. As they entered, they were confronted by an unnerving sight.

A bald man, covered from head to toe in dried blood, was sitting on the floor in the center of a five pointed star made of black rose petals. He was rocking back and forth, laughing hysterically, as he stared at a wall that had what appeared to be an outline of a body drawn on it with chalk. The expression on his face was not one of pain or fear, but of what could only be described as acceptance.

THE DANGEROUS MR. JANGLES

No one in the small town of Lynn, Massachusetts knew his name. They just called him Mr. Jangles due to the sound his cart made as he pushed it up and down the street. He was known to fix any item that was broken in return for money or food. He was, by the name of the trade, a Tinker.

The Revolutionary War had not started yet, and Great Britain still had power over her colonies. It wasn't uncommon to see many individuals offering the same kind of service as Mr. Jangles. What was uncommon was that Mr. Jangles was a black male in his early thirties.

Once the slave of a wealthy land owner, Mr. Jangles had procured his freedom by saving the man's daughter from drowning. Unfortunately, during that time period there was a price for freedom. Being a black male without any money or any place to live and only a sheet of paper declaring he was freed, truly meant nothing.

Why did the landowner, if he was so grateful to Mr. Jangles, free him but give him no money or shelter until he could make it on his own? Suspicion and rumors that Mr. Janglers was sleeping with the landowner's wife made the decision easy.

As he was walking towards town, thinking about how he was going to survive through the upcoming winter months, Mr. Jangles stumbled upon an old man fixing a broken wheel on a pushcart. Mr. Jangles quickly offered the man his assistance, seeing an opportunity to earn a meal.

When the job was completed, not only did the old man provide Mr. Jangles with a meal, but he offered him a job as his assistant, which Mr.

Jangles agreed to immediately.

As the months passed, the old man taught Mr. Jangles all the tricks of the trade in becoming a good Tinker. With the assistance of Mr. Jangles, the old man made double what he would have normally in that time period.

Sadly, when the winter months arrived, during a trip to a neighboring town, the old man collapsed and died on the road during their return. With a sad heart, Mr. Jangles carried the old man into the woods and attempted to bury him.

Even with a shovel, the ground was hard to dig into, so the old man's grave was shallow. Mr. Jangles vowed to return at the end of winter to properly bury the kind old man.

Throughout the final months of winter, it was a daily ritual to the townspeople of Lynn, Massachusetts to hear the jangle of the pushcart. No one knows who came up with the nickname, Mr. Jangles, but whenever a person needed an item fixed and heard the pushcart, they'd run to the front door and holler his name. This would always bring a wide smile to Mr. Jangles face.

Happiness, and life itself, never last long, which Mr. Jangles learned quickly.

A week before the last day of winter, a merchant wagon rolled into town bringing with it the dead body of the old man. Apparently, the merchant had discovered the old man's body when he entered the woods to relieve himself. The shallow grave had been unearthed by an animal of some kind that must have been desperate for food due to the winter and gorged itself on the remains of the old man.

When the merchant pulled back the blanket to show the townspeople his gruesome discovery, a mob quickly assembled with a united cry for justice to be dealt upon the old man's murderer. It didn't take the mob long to find Mr. Jangles. His cart was parked in front of a house where he was fixing a family's windchimes. He had just placed the chimes on a hook on the front porch when the mob swarmed him. He was beaten unmercifully and dragged to a nearby tree where the mob stood him on a chair and placed a noose around his neck.

As the leader of the mob, which just so happened to be his old master, told him the charges against him, Mr. Jangles desperately professed his innocence. Mr. Jangles sobbed uncontrollably as he told the mob how much he loved the old man and would never have hurt him. He begged them not to kill him and swore that his soul would forever seek vengeance on the town for this injustice. It was at that moment, just as Mr. Jangles uttered his curse, that his old master kicked the chair out from under him.

On the anniversary of his death, a fog rolled into town at nightfall. Throughout the night blood-curdling screams could be heard. In the morning, the surviving townspeople emerged from their houses and discovered entire families brutally murdered. Whatever committed this monstrous act by-passed any home that had a wind chime hanging on its porch.

"This has happened every year since the hanging of Mr. Jangles and still continues to this day."

Jesse Underhill stared at the elderly black man who sat across the table and smiled. He and his family had moved to the City of Lynn two months ago. As they were moving into their house, the elderly man appeared. He had introduced himself as Ephram Holmes and brought a welcoming present. The gift was a windchime, which his mother never liked. She graciously thanked him, and as he turned to leave, chucked the gift into the rubbish.

Jesse, being new to the city, befriended Ephram and visited his home often. He enjoyed the old man's stories, but this one was ridiculous.

'What's wrong?" Ephram asked.

"Well. for one, you said the town of Lynn," Jesse chuckled. "This is a city."

"It didn't become a city until much later," Ephram shrugged.

"So you expect me to believe everyone in the city puts windchimes on their porches to ward off a ghost."

"Not the whole city, only this street and the three next to it make up the original township," Ephram sighed.

"Come on Ephram, let's be real about this," Jesse said as he looked at him skeptically. "That's just some made-up ghost story to scare children."

"No, you're wrong. The story's true and you're a fool not to believe me."

"And why should I believe such a story?"

"Because it's being told to you by the direct descendent of the bastard child sired by the landowner's wife and Mr. Jangles," Ephram replied angrily.

Jesse rose from his chair as he looked out the kitchen window. "Well, thanks for the story Ephram, but it's getting late and I have to go."

As Jesse made his way to the front door, Ephram looked over at the window into the foggy night sky. Ephram's head quickly snapped over to the calendar on the wall. It was March 1st, Mr. Jangles' anniversary. He'd been so preoccupied as of late that he didn't keep track of the days. He cursed at himself for being so stupid.

"Jesse, for God's sake stay on the porch," Ephram yelled as he sprang up from his chair and raced to the front door.

When he swung open the door, the jangle of numerous windchimes filled the night air. Jesse was standing on the porch staring at something in the fog. As Ephram stood next to him, he saw what it was, the silhouette of a man pushing a cart.

"You've got to be friggin' kidding me," Jesse said looking at Ephram in disbelief. "The story was real."

Ephram nodded as they both watched the silhouette continue up the street. When it was directly in front of Jesse's house the silhouette walked away from the cart and towards Jesse's house.

"The windchimes, I gave your family windchimes," Ephram said as he grabbed Jesse by the shoulders and spun him to face him. "What happened to the windchimes?"

"My mom threw them away." Jesse replied with a look of terror on his face.

Jesse pulled away from Ephram and tried to run from the porch to his house. Ephram quickly grabbed him in a bear hug, and if Jesse had voiced any objections, they went unheard.

The only thing Ephram could hear was the tortured screams of Jesse's dying parents.

THE LAST DANCE

The cigarette smoke drifted into the night sky looking like gray fingers. James watched as it twisted and turned, then disappeared. As his eyes tracked the next tendrils of smoke, he noticed the dark silhouette of High rock Tower. He had walked up the long granite stairway leading from Essex Street to the base of the tower, but turned off before he reached it because it was a short cut to the dance hall. People claimed the number of stairs always grew when someone died at the tower, new death, new stair! He never really paid attention to how close the dance hall was to the legendary tower. He came to the dance hall every week and realized all he had to do was walk a few feet from the dance hall door and up a rocky incline and he'd be standing at the tower door. He remembered or thought he remembered hearing that the tower was built by a famous singing family during the Revolutionary War. A person standing at the top of the tower could see for miles and miles. This was probably a key lookout point for the Minutemen of Lynn, Massachusetts against any British army movements.

A prominent Minister believed the peak on which the tower was built was full of paranormal energy and with the permission of the family that owned the property built a machine called the Spirit Machine. This machine was believed by the Minister and his followers to harness the paranormal energy and bring forth a New Messiah into the world. The machine didn't work of course, but James thought of the tower's history. For a long time the tower was open for people to enjoy the view. Many picnic tables were added around the base for families to enjoy themselves. However, it was now closed to the public and for a very good reason. Over the years many people for various tragic reasons climbed the tower's stairs and instead of enjoying the view, jumped to their deaths. This had been going on since the tower was first built and was made of wood. So James had no doubt that there was some kind of supernatural energy connected to this property.

James was only eighteen years old and hadn't had much luck with dating girls as of yet. With his long black and blue eyes, he was considered to be attractive by girls his own age. He had dated a few girls on and off, but nothing was ever very serious. Many girls often flirted with him, but the turn off for them was his I don't give a crap what anybody thinks of me attitude. He refused to fall victim to the stupidity of being what others deemed fashionable and keeping up with the latest styles.he wore black—black pants, black shirts, and black sneakers. He shunned the popular kids and made it a point to avoid any event held by the so-called "in crowd." That was a job for his best friend Conner. Conner was the poster boy for the "in crowd."

He wore clothes that were only in style and never anything twice in a month. The collars of his dress shirts were perfectly pressed and clothes ironed to perfection. His pants always had a stylish pleat and his sneakers were the newest, most popular brand name. His blonde hair was short cut, spiked on top and slicked down on the sides. He was on the football team, the track team and field team, and was a shoe-in for most popular in the school year book.

They had been friends since elementary school, and he was the cause of James' inner sadness. All his parents would ever say was, "Why can't you be more like Conner," or "Conners a son any parent would be proud of." He hated to admit it, but those comments by his parents hurt him deeply.

He doubted that his parents would want him to be just like Conner if they knew the truth about him. Conner was a conceited jerk and a down right heartless individual. He had seen Conner kick a puppy repeatedly to see if he could make the puppy piss blood. He tried to stop him, but Conner had always been bigger and stronger than him. The only thing he achieved in that incident was getting himself pinned against the wall and told, "You could take the puppy's place if you'd like." That was an awful thing to witness, but even worse was how he treated girls. On occasion he was dating a girl named Renee. She was skinny with short brown hair and green eyes. While he was drinking at a party one night, just to show his control over her, he made her bark like a dog. He told her if she didn't do it that he would break up with her. He couldn't help but feel bad for the poor girl. Within everybody at the party watching, she began to bark. If that wasn't enough to humiliate her, he told her that she wasn't barking loud enough and made her increase the volume so the whole party could hear her. If his parents learned how Conner really was, he bet they'd thank their lucky stars to have him as a son.

He tossed the cigarette he was holding to the ground and stepped on it to put it out. He could hear the steady booming of the music from the Music Hall. He turned to open the door and return to the mayhem of the controlled chaos known as dancing when someone spoke.

"Why aren't you inside dancing?" A soft spoken voice asked.

When he turned, he saw a beautiful red haired girl in a black dress. Her hair was long and moving with the wind. She didn't appear to be wearing any make-up, but she honestly didn't need any because she was extremely pretty.

"Well, I, aaahhhh...," he stammered as he tried not to sound foolish, but horribly failed.

"My names Neicci," she said with a smile. "Nice to meet you, Welliaaahhh!"

"No, my name's James," he replied blushing. "I was just about to go inside. Would you like to accompany me?"

103

"Why thank you, James," she said as she walked past him as he held the door open for her to go inside.

His mouth hung open in awe as he watched her pass him. There was nothing really special about the black dress she was wearing. What was special was how it contoured her body. And what a body, he thought to himself.

The inside of the Music Hall was dark and very cramped. The tables had been pulled from the center of the area to create a dance floor. The one time picture perfect seekers of social acceptance no longer looked as pristine as they did when they first arrived. Many were now looking very sweaty from dancing and their clothing had become very wrinkled. He realized that the night was about to end and the Dance Hall was closing soon. Neicci dragged him onto the dance floor so they could dance the last dance of the night together. Looking around at all the other girls with their makeup and stylish new clothes, he knew something that they all also knew by the looks on their faces. No matter what they did or how much they spent they would never be able to replicate the natural beauty Neicci possessed.They stopped in front of the DJ table and began to dance as the final song of the night began to play.

"This song sounds nice," she said as she leaned closer into him as they swayed to the music.

"It's Journey's Open Arms," he replied. "Haven't you ever heard it before? I mean, it's been out for quite some time and is very popular."

"No," she said, sounding sad. "I must have missed it, but I'm glad they played it for my last dance."

"You're awfully cold. And you seem like you're deep in thought. Are you okay? Was someone supposed to meet you here and didn't show up or something?" He asked, trying to keep the hope that she wasn't expecting anybody out of his voice.

"No, nothing like that. I was just waiting for someone to invite me in to share the last dance of the night with me, that's all," she said in a soft voice.

"I would have definitely asked you, if I saw you," a voice said from behind them. James immediately recognized the voice and knew who it was before he even turned around.

"May I cut in?" Conner asked, smiling and looking at Neicci like a predator to a cornered prey.

"No!" James said through clenched teeth. "She's not interested!'

"I believe the choice is actually up to the lady," Conner said, holding out his hand as if there was no doubt in his mind she would rather dance with him then James.

"I'm fine right where I am, thank you," she said, leaning harder into James. "I just want to enjoy this last dance if you don't mind."

"Sure, sure," Conner said as he started to ease away from them. "Maybe we can hook-up later? You know, to talk or something, get to know one another better."

James lost sight of Conner as he melted into the crowd of onlookers. Conner was someone who always got his way, so James wasn't sure how he would handle this rejection by Neicci.

Neither of them spoke as they held each other and danced. At some point during the dance, he put his black jacket around her shoulders to help warm her up. As the song came to an end, tears formed in her eyes as she took off his jacket and returned it to him.

"So can I get your cell phone number?" James asked with a big smile on his face. "I mean, if that's okay with you?"

"I...," she started to say, with a confused look on her face. "I'm sorry. I have to go. Thank you for the last dance!"

He watched as she turned and headed for the exit. He wanted to chase after her, but what would be the point? Even though she didn't actually say, "no," that deer in the headlight look she gave him when he asked for her number. And her quick exit said it all.

As she exited the building, a hand wrapped around her waist. Conner began tugging on her and dragging her along towards the rocky hill leading up to High Rock Tower.

"What are you doing?" she asked angrily. "I have to go, the last dance has ended. You're ruining everything!"

"Oh calm down, drama queen," he said, leading her forcefully up the hill. "I just want to talk to you in private for a minute or two."

"I have to go! You don't understand," she cried out hysterically.

"Look, we're just going to the top of the tower to enjoy the view and get to know each other better. No harm. No foul! You might even enjoy yourself," Conner said with a devious smile as they got closer to the tower door.

"The tower is closed to the public. It's locked," she said with tears running down her face and a scared look washed over her face. "Please, I don't want to go up there!"

"The locks have been broken off for a while now. We come here sometimes during the weekends to hang out and drink beers." Conner said, as he opened the tower door and pulled her inside. She tugged at his hand as they climbed the stone stairs, but his hold was just too strong. When they got to the top of the stairs there was a ladder that led to the very top of the tower, he had her climb up first. Once they were both through the opening in the roof, he closed the metal trap door.

"Come here and look at how cool the view is," he said as he moved to the edge of the tower.

"No!" She yelled, as she tried to make it to the trap door, but he was too quick and beat her there easily.

"Look, just relax and try to enjoy yourself," he said, faking a smile. "I only want to talk to you for a few minutes. Get to know you a little more about you. Then you can go. I promise!"

"I can't be here, please," she sobbed, placing both of her hands over her face and shaking it back and forth as if she was fighting a headache. "I just wanted my last dance!"

"What's wrong with you? You have some mental illness or something?" He asked, looking at Neicci as if she was an escapee from an insane asylum. "I mean seriously, what's the big deal about being up here?"

"I was up here once before with my boyfriend at the time. His name was Todd. He told me that he wanted to bring me up here and show me something amazing! He promised me we'd make it back before the last dance of the evening," she said with tears streaming down her face.

"So what did he show you?" He asked, his curiosity now peaked. "I mean, can I see it from here, or was it something private?"

"No, I'll show you," she said with a smile as she moved to the very edge of the tower.

"So what did he show you that was so amazing?" He asked, as he stepped to the edge with her.

"How the ground seems to just rise up to meet you," she screamed, as her cold, dead hands shoved him off the top of the tower!

James heard the scream and looked back up the stone staircase towards High Rock Tower. The stairs seemed to fade in and out and he wasn't sure but it seemed there was another step at the top. He shook his head, "Stupid imagination," he said out loud, the dark silhouette of the tower against the moonlight sky always creeped him out.

DISGRUNTLED

Kim sat in her car and watched and Alan headed towards the dark grocery store. A few other employees left their cars and followed after him. This meant he was the manager on duty this morning and he was a nice enough guy, but he didn't do well assigning people to sections. He totally failed at placing your aces in the right places. She grabbed her apron, box cutter, and name badge and left her car making the walk to the store's front doors. This was her first day back after being suspended for three days and of course her return fell on a Friday. She was suspended due to a confrontation with a customer. The thing was there was truly no confrontation. A customer asked her if there was any half gallon whole milk because the shelf was empty. She was the one who stocked the box that morning and knew there wasn't anymore, they only got shipped one crate. She explained this to the customer and when she was done the customer said, "Can you just go check out back." She said, "No," and again explained that she knew that there wasn't any out back and to have her go look would be a waste of time and she was a little busy still getting the store stocked from the morning truck. She left the customer and went about stocking the shelves and after about five minutes she was being called over the store intercom to report to the manager's office. When she got there the customer was out in front of the office with the manager and as she approached the customer pointed at her and said, "That's her, she said I was wasting her time and she was too busy to help me. If that's the type of service you encourage your employees to have towards your customers I'll take my business someplace else."

The store manager assured the customer it wasn't and told her to apologize immediately. Her anger got the better of her and she flat out refused and called the customer a pathetic liar and a miserable human being. If it had been at any other time that would have cost her her job, but the store was seriously understaffed and losing a good worker needed to be avoided at all cost. So instead of being fired she was suspended for three days and a further review of the situation was pending.

So as she entered the store and closed the doors behind her she made up her mind that she had had enough. If the company she had worked for the last three years was just going to take the word of a customer over hers and suspend her without pay. Then her time here was just about done. She felt over worked, underpaid, and worst off unappreciated.

"Hey Kim," she heard Alan say as she approached the time clock to punch in.

"So I have good news and bad news. First the truck is going to be about a half hour late. So it'll be here around 5:30 am, which still gives us plenty of time because we don't open until 8:00 am. Unfortunately, we had three call outs and it's just going to be you and me in the Box. I'm going to need everyone else to break down the dry food pallets and refrigerated vegetable pallets."

Kim knew that what he was truly saying was "you're screwed and I'll make an appearance here and there and maybe touch a milk or yogurt pallet, but don't hold your breath." Since she hadn't been in in a few days there was no telling how bad the Box truly was. Did the night crew have time to go in the Box and work the back stock? Did they only pull a few items forward and make it look presentable or did they properly face the Box? All this raced through her head as she stared at Alan wanting to wipe that stupid grin off his face.

"That's fine," she said as she walked past him headed to the Box to see exactly what she was up against this morning.

As she lifted the cold shades she could tell the night crew must have been busy or at least she hoped that was the case because the Box was a mess. The milks, yogurts, eggs, and juices were all in disarray. There was an apple left by someone just sitting on an egg carton, whoever closed the shade must have just been like the hell with it they can deal with it in the morning.

That was one of Kim's true pet peeves about working in a grocery store, people leaving products wherever they felt. It was just such a waste sometimes, she'd find fresh fruit or other refrigerated products discarded in the frozen section. These products were now unusable and had to be written off and thrown out. She laughed as she remembered overhearing two lady customers complaining that other countries call Americans lazy. Then these same ladies instead of going back and putting a cake back where they got it placed in on a chip shelf two aisles over. Kim wanted to grab the cake and go over to the ladies and say, "Other countries aren't wrong." but she didn't. She just picked up the cake and put it back where it belonged, today however that may end up going a totally different way!

She finished facing the Box and working the back stock before the truck actually arrived. Another associate named Patrick was the one who would help unload the truck and bring the pallets of product in. Kim knew that the truck load would be big because it was Friday and the start of the weekend. Which is when a large majority of people go food shopping. Once the truck was completely unloaded there were a total of five pallets for the Box, one pallet of eggs, one of milk, and three with a variety of yogurts, juices, and other products. If Alan actually helped this wouldn't have been too bad, however, since they were short staffed she barely saw him. He came in the back room and took a few things off a pallet and put them on flat carts then was called out to the floor and didn't return. Definitely not how she wanted to start her first day back.

She managed to actually get everything broken down, put up and back stock put away with ten minutes to spare before the store opened. She walked into the break room and grabbed herself a coffee. She was taking a ten minute break. Hell, she basically got the whole Box done by herself and was tired.

"Here you are, we did it! Great Job." He said proudly as he made himself a cup of coffee and sat across from her. "I had to start you on the register, sorry!"

It took Kim everything in her power not to ask him what he meant by we did it. Did he have an ant in his pocket, because there was no we did anything, it was more to the effect she did it.

THE REGISTER

Most of the morning shoppers were older. They knew what they wanted, where it was and how much exactly they were spending. For the most part they were nice, but there of course were the ones who were just constantly in a bad mood. The morning shopping crowd is for the most part more relaxed, it has a less rushed vibe. Around 11:00 am you can actually feel the vibe change, there's more customers in the building, people are in every aisle, there's a sort of tension in the building. The odd thing is, when one person goes to check out it's like a domino effect and all of a sudden there's huge lines at the registers and every cashier is turning on their lights for assistance.

A customer with a cart full of groceries came to Kims line. She sighed, being short staffed she knew she wasn't going to have a bagger and this customer had already set the tone of the transaction. Kim was told to be sure that she put the frozen with the frozen, the refrigerated with the refrigerated, and so on. Honestly, a valid request, but then the customer had to say, "Do you think you can handle that!" Kim's eye's narrowed as she shrugged off the blatant disrespectful comment and started ringing up the product on the conveyor belt and putting them in bags.

"Did you check your eggs," Kim asked, opening the egg carton for inspection.

"Why?" the customer asked, annoyed.

"To check and see if any are broken or cracked." Kim said with a smile.

"Isn't that your job! Shouldn't you be doing that before you sell them." The customer said clearly becoming even more annoyed.

Kim finished checking the eggs and put them on top of one of the bags. In her mind she thought, sure we have so much free time to assign someone to go through all cartons of eggs when they come in on the pallets, but said nothing and kept ringing up the order.

Kim grabbed a lemon and looked for a bar code and there wasn't one stuck on the fruit. She looked at the register for a product list, but there was none, so she turned on the light to blink indicating she needed assistance.

"What's the problem?"

"There's no barcode on the fruit for me to scan, so I need someone to get me the PLU Number." Kim explained.

"It's a Lemon." the customer said, pointing out the obvious.

KIm's mind raced, did this customer just mansplain a lemon to me. I know it's a damn lemon, but I need the PLU number because I don't know the price, she thought to herself.

"Yes I know it's a lemon, but there's a number I need to ring it in." Kim said, trying to act cheerful.

"I didn't know that you needed to be a Rocket Scientist to work here," the customer said in a belittling tone.

Kim finished the transaction and wasn't at all sad to see the customer leave. The customer clearly did not want to be shopping and felt that taking out their frustrations on her with insults would make shopping better.

After that customer left she had a bunch of good customers who joked and laughed with her. These were the customers that made the day easier, they understood that the store wasn't full staffed and weren't trying to make her job more stressful.

She had five minutes left on her register hour and a customer pushed a full cart into her register. The customer was on the phone and when Kim greeted them they just kept talking on the phone. Normally the customer put the product on the conveyor belt, but his customer turned their back on her and kept talking on the phone. Kim rang everything up and bagged it, placing the bags back in the cart and then told the customer the total.

"SHHHH," the customer said, holding up their finger indicating in just one minute. "This is an important phone call."

The customer continued to talk on the phone and now a small line of other customers formed behind them wanting to check out. Kim was beyond frustrated at how rude this customer just acted towards her and decided to respond to them in an equally petty, but self satisfying way.

"What was that now?" The customer asked after ending their phone call.

"One second," Kim said, holding up her finger to the customer and pretending to be checking the wiring on the cash register. The customer's facial expression became one of anger, but what could they honestly say to her. Kim happily took the customers money after a few minutes and watched as they threw the receipt in the bag and stormed out.

"Have a nice day!" Kim shouted out after them, clearly poking the bear.

Kim's relief came and she was beyond happy to get off the register, she was already all peopled out and the day was still young. Janice, another employee who was on register, walked beside her as they headed out back to look at the board to see what still needed to be done in the store for stocking.

"Getting busy." Janice said with indifference in her voice.

"Yeah, typical Friday," Kim replied with a shrug of her shoulders.

"No matter how busy we get it'll compare to when covid first started, remember." Janice said, shaking her head at the memory.

"Oh, I remember," Kim said, there wasn't a person in the world who could possibly forget, especially the workers that were deemed Essential Workers.That meant essentially you were the only contact these people would have and have to deal with their frustrations. Doctors, Nurses, Pharmacist, and Grocery Store workers.

They were the only ones allowed to stay open during the Pandemic. They were the front line, and therefore the only ones who would be the brunt of people's fears and frustrations.

COVID 19: THE PANDEMIC

When news hit that essential everything would be locked down and due to no one being allowed in or out of the country it became a shit show. With the knowledge that food and other supplies may be hard to obtain, people panicked. Kim worked that first week and it was insane! Customers rushed in and bought everything they could get their hands on. Kim Watched one customer go to a stand up freezer and pull all the frozen broccoli from it into their cart. Customers were hoarding toilet paper, hand sanitizer, bottled water, and cleaning supplies without a care for anyone else. The shelves of the store at the end of the night were totally bare. Kim saw things purchased in abundance that she knew hardly ever sold before this happened. When a product ran out on the shelves the customers refused to believe there was none out back. Some even made crazy accusations that the company was holding it from them in order to hike up the price.

The store workers were given a choice: they could stay and work through this awful time or go on unemployment. At the time nothing was truly known about Covid except that if you got it the chances of you dying was extremely high and there was no cure. Many employees chose to go the unemployment route and Kim totally understood why. The decision to stay and work through this situation was a hard one for sure. Many employees had elderly family members who lived with them or small children. Did they really want to take the chance of working and bringing a potentially deadly disease home to their loved ones, highly unlikely. Kim lived alone and didn't have to face that problem, so she chose to stay and work.

The stores eventually gained some assemblance of order. They put a limit on the amount of one product a person could buy, especially toilet paper. They drew or taped boxes six feet away from the registers and put up plexiglass to protect the cashiers, the put arrows in the aisles indicating to walk one way, mask were required in the store, and a limit of how many people could be in the store at one time was put in place. The stores assigned staff to stay at the front doors and count how many people were in the stores and ask people to please wait outside and form an orderly line until they could enter. Carriages were the only thing customers were allowed to use at first, this was they could pass the carriage to the cashier and maintain the six foot social distance requirement. The carriages were wiped down with alcohol wipes after every use so they would be fresh for the next customer. This truly was well thought out and devised to keep the customers safe and able to shop without having to fear someone coming within their six foot bubble.

The problem with it was simple, people! Most people are accustomed to doing whatever they want and don't want to be told or follow any simple rules. Especially from someone they feel is less than them and many view retail workers as pathetic subservients.

So to have one of these employees tell them what to do caused more problems then you could possibly imagine. Most of the customers were appreciative of the precautions the store put in place for their safety and the safety of their employees. However, there's what Kim liked to call, "The Entitled." These were the customers who would walk up to the door past the long line of people waiting and ask, "I'm only getting one item, do I seriously have to wait in that line?" When the person working the door said, "Yes," they would become verbally abusive and storm off either to wait in line or go somewhere else. Some customers would just storm past the door employee despite being told there was a waiting line. Some would refuse to wear a mask inside the store. Many would lie and say they had a medical condition and couldn't wear a mask or it was against their religious beliefs. You are forbidden by law to ask for proof on either of these reasons to be excluded from the mask mandate. Many of these customers would clearly be lying, but what could you do? When they would enter the store customers who were wearing masks would protest them being in the store, but a manager would have to tell them by law they have to be allowed entrance.

The store told the door workers if they saw an elderly customer waiting in line to bring them to the front. They didn't want an elderly customer standing out in the hot sun, pouring rain, or freezing cold. This only caused a problem on one occasion that Kim knew of and of course she was the employee on the door. It was a hot day and the store had her passing out cold waters to anyone waiting in line who wanted one. She saw the elderly customer and started escorting her to the front of the line. The majority of people waiting in line were sympathetic and didn't have an issue with it, but there's always one! The customer stepped out of line and began complaining about having to wait and how ridiculous this whole setup was. The customer demanded to know why Kim was showing favoritism to this customer just because they were old. Many people waiting had health issues and why weren't they brought to the front of the line. Kim ignored the customer and refused to engage in a confrontation and continued leading the elderly customer to the head of the line.

"The customers are always right." the customer began shouting.

Kim truly hated that people used that and truly had no clue what it meant! That phrase dealt with pricing and quality issues and did not give customers the right to abuse employees. When the complaining customer got to the front of the line he looked at Kim and said, "I wish I had Covid so I could spit in your face!"

That was it for Kim as a person monitoring the door. She went to the manager and told him about the man's comments. With all the reported violence against grocery store workers doing their jobs across the country she just didn't want to be in that situation ever again. The manager totally understood and apologized to her for having to experience that.

If anything the Covid 19: Pandemic showed Kim how truly selfish and mean people had become towards one another. There was a time when it was Love Thy Neighbor. That time had sadly passed and the new trend was Hooray for me and the Hell with you!

REALITY

Once Kim finished reflecting on what it was like working at this store during the pandemic she realized a reality. The reality was that the company, despite knowing all that its employees had to deal with during the pandemic, wasn't appreciated. They had no problem believing the customer who complained about her and suspending her. However, the customer who actually threatened her wasn't spoken to or asked to leave. They allowed that customer to go about their business and shop despite what they had said to her. Therein lies the problem, companies coddle customers bad behavior due to the fear of them not returning or giving the store a bad review. All a customer has to do is raise their voice and stomp their feet like a spoiled child and a company bends over backwards for them. Yet if you're an employee, an actual worker for the company and bust your ass day in and day out for them you truly mean nothing to them! You can be replaced easily is clearly their mindset.

"Do you work here?" Kim heard a customer ask, snapping her out of her inner venting session.

In Kim's mind she thought to herself. Why no, I'm a spy from another grocery store who gave me this name tag and apron with the company's logo on it. This is all an evil plot by my true company to have me infiltrate and steal this company's secrets.

"Yes, actually I do. How can I help you," Kim said, faking a smile.

"I'm looking for a gallon of whole milk and there's none on the shelf. Could you be a dear and go out back and see if there's any more.

Kim already knew the answer to this because she was the one who unloaded the pallets and stocked and back stocked the Box. She was about to explain this to the customer, but caught herself and remembered how she got suspended.

"Sure, absolutely, I'll be right back," Kim said as she headed to the back room.

Once inside the Box Kim just stood there and felt the cold air rush over her. It was actually pretty refreshing, the day was hot and after thinking about everything that had happened she was getting a little hot under the collar as they say. So the coolness of the Box had a rather calming effect on her. She didn't actually look to see if there were any gallons of whole milk, she again already knew the answer. As long as the customer believed she looked that was all that could be expected of her.

When she came back out onto the floor the customer was gone. Kim hated when a customer did this. They'd ask a question then wander off and now she would have to search the store trying to find them and give them the answer. She eventually found the customer a few aisles over talking to another employee named John.

"Kim, I was just coming to find you. This customer is looking to see if we have any gallons of whole milk in the back because there's none on the shelf." John said as she approached.

"Yes we actually already spoke and I told you I would go look for you," Kim said as nicely as she possibly could despite being a little angry.

"I just thought you had forgotten or were too busy to look for me." the customer said nonchalantly.

"Well I did look for you and unfortunately we're out for the day, but we'll have more first thing in the morning." Kim said.

"Tomorrow morning, well that really doesn't help me now dear does it. I guess I'll just have to go somewhere else to get it!" The customer said as if asking Kim and John this question was a total waste of the customers time. The customer turned and walked away without even a thank you for looking.

"Why do customers do that?" John asked, clearly frustrated by the interaction with the customer.

"You mean ask several different employees the same question." Kim asked sarcastically.

"Yeah it's beyond frustrating! What are they expecting? That they'll get a better answer than the one they are going to get from you." John said in a disgusted tone.

"Yes, that is 100 percent what it is and don't let it get to you." Kim said as she walked away to go back to see what needed to be done.

Other employees slowly started trickling in as the day wore on. The store became more and more busier to the point that the aisles were cramped and hard to walk down. Covid was still a thing, but with the vaccinations and boosters it wasn't as strict as in the beginning. People didn't have to wear masks anymore; it wasn't a requirement, but some customers still did. It was over two years ago that the pandemic started and many things had gotten back to somewhat normal. The restrictions were lifted so there was no more limit on the amount of customers in the store at once. The plexiglass and boxes were removed, six foot distancing was no longer required, but some people still did it just to be safe. One thing that stuck out to Kim was how bad children behaved. She was no child specialist, but it seemed as if with them unable to attend school or see their friends that their social skills were definitely lacking. This was especially noticeable when they were out shopping, they seemed to be just unleashing frustration and energy. The effects on the children because of being locked in their houses for so long without contact with other people would last a while, she thought to herself.

Kim took her lunch every day she worked around 11:30 am. Her normal shift was from 5:00am to 1:00pm, usually five days a week. She liked taking her lunch later and once lunch was over she only had an hour left on her shift. When she came back from lunch she noticed that on the to-do board no one had marked off that they were doing a frozen pull. She cut a piece of cardboard off a box that was sticking out of the bailer and went out and wrote a list of things she could fill. After she went into the freezer and loaded a flat cart with the items she could find that needed to be stocked then she pushed her cart onto the sales floor. As she turned her cart into one of the frozen aisles a customer began flagging her down.

"Excuse me, can I ask you a question, please!" the customer asked with a big smile.

"How can I help," Kim said, looking at the customer and realizing that she actually knew this customer.

Kim had dealt with this customer once before. During the start of the pandemic this customer refused to put on a mask when asked and told Kim she was just a sheep for doing what the government told her to do. This customer went on and on about how Covid wasn't real and it was nothing but a ploy by the government to control us and take away our rights. When Kim told her that her company mandated that they wear masks and since she was an employee of the company would do whatever they told her to do. The customer shouted that she was nothing but a follower and what this country needed was leaders as she stormed out of the store.

Now almost two years removed, the customer was in front of her asking her to help with something.

"Have you tried this?" The customer asked, holding up a bag of Chinese chicken.

"Yes and I thought it was disgusting!" Kim said and made a facial expression to emphasize her opinion.

"The website I follow says it's incredible," the customer said looking at Kim confused by the answer she gave her.

"So you're taking advice from a website you follow," Kim emphasized the sentence on purpose.

"Yes, I've been following their suggestions for a while and they've been correct on their suggestions for the most part," the customer said, turning the package and reading the ingredients.

"Well, my suggestion to you would be to make your own decision about it. I personally didn't like it, but if you choose to follow other people's suggestions that's up to you," Kim said again emphasizing the sentence on purpose.

"Okay thank you!" the customer said, totally oblivious to Kims subtle jabs about being a follower.

As she was finishing up and about to push the flat cart into the back room Janice walked up to her.

"You know they've been watching you all day right." Janice said, looking at Kim with concern.

"Who? Who's been watching me?" Kim asked, confused.

"The Store Manager and Regional Manager, they've been up in the office watching you from the window," Janice said motioning with her head towards the two way mirror on the second floor where the manager's office was located.

"Wait, you knew about this and didn't tell," Kim said in frustration.

"We all did, but we didn't want to get involved, sorry!" Janice said sadly as she walked away.

Well this is just great Kim thought to herself, what else could possibly go wrong today! The Universe must have heard her and said, here hold my beer and watch, because once that thought entered her mind she was being paged to the Manager's office over the store intercom.

THE END OF THE SHIFT

Kim walked through the store towards the stairs that led up to the Manager's office. In her mind she already had her. I don't need this job speech planned out. If this was how they were going to be towards her then fine they could fire her, she was done taking anymore crap from them and these self entitled customers. She at least worked during her shift! Hell half the new hires couldn't be found half the time. She even found one hiding in a circle of boxes in the back room texting on her phone. Yet she was the one they were going to fire because some customer lied due to the fact they didn't get their way. This was just such bullshit, she thought as she bound up the stairs to the office!

There was no door at the top of the stairs so when Kim arrived there she could see directly into the office. Standing in front of the large window looking over the sales floor was the Store Manager Mark and another man. They must have heard her coming up the stairs because they both turned towards her once she reached the door.

"Kim, please come in. Have you met our Regional Manager before? This is Mr. Jackson," Mark said as he gestured towards the other man in the office.

"You can call me Kevin," the Regional Manager said in a friendly voice. "I'm here following up on a customer complaint and your suspension."

"I...," Kim started to speak but was cut off by Kevin.

"Please allow me to finish," Kevin said.

Kim hated that! Why do people think it's okay to just cut someone off when they clearly have something important to add to the conversation. She could feel herself getting anxious, she was going to unload all of her frustrations on them once they dropped the hammer on her.

"So, in regards to this complaint it seems there's been a few new developments. The customer who complained about you did almost the exact same thing in another one of our stores. It appears this customer has a track record of actually doing this to our employees if the customer isn't catered hand and foot by us." Kevin said in a tone that to Kim sounded like him apologizing in a way.

"You're saying this customer has done this repeatedly and it wasn't noticed until now. How many employees have lost pay or been fired due to a customer that blatantly lies to get their way. Is this customer being banned from our stores." Kim said angrily.

"No, we try to maintain great customer relations. We spoke with the customer and informed them that we are now aware of their repeated false accusations and will no longer act upon them." Kevin said as if this made everything better.

"Am I or any of the other employees who have been suspended being issued checks for the wages we lost due to this customer. Is the company hiring back anyone who was fired due to this customer's lies." Kim said, trying to hold back the fury she felt inside her at what had been revealed to her.

"No, the company does not hold itself at fault for doing its best to maintain a strong customer relations brand." Kevin said with a stone expression on his face.

"So that's it!" Kim said, clearly frustrated.

"Not exactly!" Kevin replied with an odd look on his face. "You've been with the company for a few years now and I was sent here to observe you as you worked."

"So you wanted to have a valid reason to fire me." Kim said disgustedly.

"No, not at all. In fact it's actually the opposite." Kevin said now with a big smile on his face. "I liked what I saw and how you went about doing your job. You are a hard worker and handle the customer very well from what I saw. I'm actually here to offer you an Assistant Manager position. Sean the night time Assistant Manager is transferring to another store and we'd like you to move up into his old position. What do you say? Are you interested?"

Kim wanted to explode! She knew that they were only offering her this position because of the mishandling of the complaint. This was the company's way of sweeping the problem under the rug. This was it, this was her chance to go off and tell them exactly what she thought of them and this job.

"How much of a pay increase is it?" Kim heard herself say. Then for some strange reason Alanis Morissette's song, Isn't it Ironic, began playing in her head.

THE DIG

E.J. tossed the dirt from the shovel and looked up from the hole at Sean and Tyree. They had been digging for a few hours now and the progress was going well.

"You really believe that digging here will allow us to get into the tunnels of Dungeon rock?" E.J. asked, looking over in Tyrees direction.

"I wouldn't have us out here doing this if I wasn't. There's way better ways to spend a Friday night." Tyree said, kneeling down to look at the hole to gauge how deep it was now.

"Hell yeah there is! We could be pounding back a few brews and hanging out with some good looking girls instead of doing this dumb shit!" Sean said looking over at Tyree annoyed.

"You won't be saying that when we break through and retrieve the pirates' treasure." Tyree replied.

"People have been trying to get into Dungeon Rock for like a hundred years. Ever since the inner entrance collapsed and trapped the pirate and his loot. What makes you think you can do better than every other treasure hunter before you?" Sean said looking over at Tyree with a smug expression on his face.

"Seriously, My intelligence is being questioned by a guy with the nickname Sparrow! How did you get that nickname again? You found a dead Sparrow as a child or something like that, right?" Tyree said sarcastically.

"No smart ass I threw a rock and hit one in mid air and killed it!" Sparrow said with a little anger in his voice.

"E.J. Are you listening to this shit! We're about to share a king's ransom in gold with a would-be bird assassin. What the fuck!" Tyree said in a mocking tone.

"Both of you knock it off. I'm not going to lie being in Lynn Woods at night and doing this is a little creepy. Let's do this shit and get the hell out of here." E.J. said clearly annoyed by his two friends bantering back and forth. "Sparrow, stop messing with Tyree and Tyree just explain why you chose this spot for us to dig in."

"Fine," Tyree said annoyed, "Okay, sometime before the 1638 earthquake a group of pirates came to Lynn. The pirates traded silver for manacles, digging tools, chains and other supplies. The area where the exchange took place is known as Pirates Glen. The four men left and then returned and one brought with him a bride. They built a small house to live in and after a few months the woman perished from fever. Then the authorities found the pirates' hideout and raided them. They arrested three of the pirates and returned them to England for prosecution.

The fourth pirate escaped into the woods and lived in a cave that the pirates excavated. It was here that he was living when the earthquake of 1638 struck. The foundation of the cave tumbled in upon him, trapping him and his treasure in what is now known as Dungeon Rock.

"We all know the legend, but why aren't we digging closer to Dungeon Rock? Why are we digging so far away from in and in the woods?" Sparrow asked, staring at Tyree like he was wasting all their time.

"I'm getting to that! just chill out!" Tyree was clearly upset about being interrupted before he could finish his explanation. "Now I'm sure you know of the Wolf Pits here in Lynn Woods. No one knows when they were dug or who did the digging. They both are both two feet wide and five feet long. However, the first is seven feet deep and the second is only five. Then despite the fact that they are called the Wolf Pits there are no records of wolves ever being in this area."

"People have been coming up with ideas on why those pits are there for years. No one knows what the hell they are for. What's that have to do with us being here?" Sparrow asked him as E.J. and he traded places so he could take over the digging.

"I think the pirates made those pits with the tools they got from the townspeople. I think those play a part in Dungeon Rock being excavated by the pirates. I honestly believe the two are connected somehow, but there's more. Stone Tower was built in these woods in 1936 and they claimed it was for fire observation purposes. Yet from the tower you get a clear view of Lynn's waterfront." Tyree was clearly excited by what he was saying.

"E.J. Are you listening to this nut job! He has us out here on some wild goose chase." Sparrow said from the hole.

"Let's hear him out before we beat his ass for having us waste our Friday night." E.J. laughed.

"Funny, you guys are a laugh, a minute." Tyree said glaring at both E.J. and Sparrow. "Now Stone Tower is forty eight feet tall, but before it was built they already had a tower. Steel Tower which was built in 1895. Steel Tower is located on Burrill Hill and is the highest point in Lynn, approximately 275 feet above sea level. FromSteel Tower you get a perfect view of all the surrounding towns and water front. This tower was also built to allegedly be used for observational purposes in case of fires. Why? Why have two towers that you're claiming serve the exact same purpose"

"Hello, because they needed an upgrade, Steel Tower was old as fuck and they wanted a newer model that's why the built Stone Tower." Sparrow yelled from the hole acting as if he was stating the blatantly obvious.

"No, these towers were built specifically to watch for something. They feared that something was coming and they wanted plenty of time to get away from whatever it was!" Tyree said with a serious voice. "Did you know that Burrill Hill isn't its original name? It was originally Mount Nebo and they changed it to Burrill Hill. The meaning of Nebo is prophesies! What prophecy is linked to this area? Do you know? Because I sure as hell don't and how bad it is that they built these towers to warn them of whatever danger that comes along with this prophecy. I drew lines from all these locations, which I'm sure are linked somehow and by my calculations they all connect here to this spot. So what do you think?" Tyree said triumphantly looking at his two friends.

E.J. and Sparrow looked at each other and began laughing hysterically. Tyree could only stare at the two in disbelief. He mapped it out for them, he couldn't have explained it any better, why on earth were they laughing at him.

"Yo E.J. don't you have a soccer game tomorrow? Maybe we call it a night and stop this foolish nonsense." Sparrow said from the hole no longer digging.

"No it's actually Sunday and we've already wasted most of the night. We might as well keep going and see what happens," E.J. said in an unenthused tone.

"Whatever," Sparrow said as resumed digging.

"Oh come on seriously what's the problem?" Tyree said in frustration.

"Honestly, You're the whitest black person I know," E.J. said in an annoyed tone.

"Hey watch that racist shit E.J." Tyree said angrily.

"Since I'm half black it's not being racist. It's stating the damn obvious. You listen to Rock and Roll music and collect comic books. Hell Sparrow is 100% white and acts blacker than you!" E.J. said, staring at Tyree.

"Word!" Sparrow said from the hole which broke the tension and caused them all to laugh.

"Guns and Roses are just bad ass by the way and I don't collect just any comic books. I collect Spiderman and any that I believe will be worth money someday." Tyree said, smiling with a justified expression on his face.

Just as he finished there was a loud moaning sound and then Sparrow was gone. E.J and Tyree couldn't see anything in the holes darkness; all they could hear was the sounds of stones crashing below.

"Ooooowww," Sparrow could be heard saying from the hole.

"Holy shit! Are you okay Sparrow?" Tyree yelled down the hole with concern.

"Yeah, I always just randomly scream out ooooowww, dumbass!" Sparrow's voice said from the darkness.

"Yup he's fine!" E.J. laughed. "Can you see anything?"

"Just you morons looking down at me, toss me down one of those flashlights and get down here! We have a treasure to find!" Sparrow replied.

They tossed down a flashlight and tied off a rope to a nearby tree so they could lower themselves down. Once they got to the bottom they could see Sparrow standing near a wall shining his flashlight on it.

"What Gives?" E.J. asked, as he walked over to see what Sparrow was looking at.

"I know why the pirates bought manacles," Sparrow said, nodding towards where he was pointing his flashlight. In the light could be seen two skeletons manacled to the stone wall.

"Tyree, there's no record of anyone getting into Dungeon Rock after the cave-in, right?" E.J. said to Tyree as he walked over to where his two friends were standing.

"Hell no! There'd be all kinds of documentation of that and there's none that I know of, Why?" Tyree said as he looked at E.J. in a curious manner.

"Because those skeletons are wearing what looks like ripped and torn blue jeans with what I think is a concert t-shirt and the one on the left appears to be wearing a Union Soldier uniform. So how is that possible?" E.J. asked, turning to Tyree for an answer.

"It's not! They shouldn't be here." Tyree said as he walked over to the skeletons to get a better look. "This skeleton with the jeans seems to be young. I'm no expert, but I'd say he was around ten or eleven years old when he died." Lee said, looking at E.J. and Sparrow.

"Wait, weren't there two friends that disappeared in the seventies? Everyone believed it was the work of those two guys who would drive around in a van wearing clown suits." Sparrow said, squinting to look at the skeleton as if he might see something that would affirm that this was in fact one of those boys.

"They never found those boys or any of the children that became missing due to those clowns.The abductions just stopped! A bunch of people thought that it was just a story made up by parents to scare their children into behaving." E.J. said moving next to Tyree as they both now stared at the skeleton intently.

"That might be the case for that skeleton, but what about this guy?" Tyree said, pointing over to the skeleton on the left. "Who the hell is he and how the Hell did they both get down here?"

"No clue! Maybe we should come back bright and early when it's light out. I think that would be our best bet." Sparrow said walking over to where the rope was hanging.

"I'm not leaving until we find the treasure. If we leave someone might stumble across that hole we made and claim our treasure and fame." Tyree said as he stood up and walked over to one of the two corridors that led out of the cave they were in.

"Yeah, I agree with Tyree. We've already come this far. Might as well see it out to the finish.' E.J. said as he walked to where Tyree was standing.

"If it'll make you feel better you can stay here and make sure nothing happens to the rope." Tyree said, looking over at Sparrow.

"Screw you, you dickless wonder! I'm not staying here alone with the dead people!" sparrow yelled walking over to Tyree angrily.

"Hey, hey chillout! There"s no need for anyone to stay with the rope. No one knows we're here, so let's all go together." E.J. said stepping in between his two friends. "We good? If so we'll head down this tunnel first if it turns out to be nothing we'll backtrack and then go down the next."

"Fine!" Tyree and Sparrow both said in unison as they all headed down the first tunnel passage.

The three friends walked for what seemed like hours. The passage was wide at some points and in others areas they were forced to walk in single file. As they turned a bend in the passage they saw a light coming from what appeared to be a room straight ahead.

"FREE ME!" A voice boomed in all their heads.

"What the fuck was that?" Tyree said, looking back and forth between E.J. and Sparrow.

"Mannnnn! I said let's leave and come back tomorrow when it was light out. Now we have some creepy spirit voice yelling at us. This is the shit I was afraid of! Now we're too far away from the rope to get the Hell out of here and too close to that room not to see the treasures in it! We're dead!" Sparrow said as he ran a finger across his throat.

"Knock that shit off and come on." E.J. said as he walked towards the room entrance.

The three friends slowly and cautiously approached the room entrance and peeked in. there didn't appear to be anybody in the room, but it was filled with an overflowing chest of treasure. They rushed in and began rummaging through the chest grabbing handfuls of treasure and stuffing their pockets.

"FREE ME!" The voice boomed in their heads again causing them to take their eyes off the treasure chest and look around the room. There floating in the air before them was a large blue crystal emanating the light in the room.

"I claim dibs!" Tyree said, walking towards the crystal.

"Yeah, that's not how that's going to work, sorry Tyree." E.J. said, staring at the crystal in awe.

"Guys what the hell is that!" Sparrow said, also staring at the crystal in awe.

"That is The Heart of The Mother!" A figure said as it stepped out from a dark corner in the room.

The three friends turned and couldn't believe what they saw standing in front of them. There in front of them was a figure that seemed to be fading in and out of focus. All of them stepped away from the figure and closer to the door they came through.The fact that the figure looked and sounded like what they always thought a pirate to be escaped none of them.

"Who the hell are you?" Sparrow said angrily.

"Who am I? Who am I? That's truly an interesting question and one I haven't been asked in a long long time. I suppose once I was a Captain of a Pirate ship named The Brightburn, but that was a long time ago. Now I'm the Trapped One." The figure said as it continued to fade in and out before them.

"Are you the one asking us to free you? You're the ghost of the pirate that got trapped here during the earthquake. Is that why you're calling yourself the Trapped One?' Tyree asked, staring at the figure now with an almost excited look on his face.

"FREE ME!" The voice echoed in their heads almost on cue.

"As you probably realize now I am not the one asking to be freed and I am the pirate you mentioned, but it's not because the earthquake trapped me here. It's because The Heart of The Mother cursed me til the end of time to be trapped between the two worlds for not freeing her son."

"What are you talking about?" E.J. asked, looking at the figure bewildered by his comments.

"Learn!" The figure said, and before anyone could react was instantly in front of E.J. and it appeared as if he stuck his spectral fingers into the temples of E.J. His head immediately snapped back and his eyes rolled into the back of his head. Sparrow and Tyree grabbed articles of treasure from the room as weapons and took defensive stances.

"Let him go! They both screamed at the figure.

"Learn!" the figure repeated staring at E.J.

E.J. had no idea what had happened one minute he was talking to the spectral figure and the next he was surrounded in darkness. He could hear the figure's voice coming out of the darkness. What was he saying? He was telling E.J. something, his story.

"The news was spreading of the Great Wryms death from the injuries she sustained in the battle with the Knight. There was nothing protecting her vast treasure with her now gone, it could be theirs. The Coalition of Pirates had to act fast before someone else caught wind of this golden opportunity. The pirates made a pact that they would all travel to the Great Wyrm's Lair and divide her treasure equally among them. The travel by sea was long and hard but eventually the twelve pirate ships that set out on this adventure spotted the Legendary Isle of Ash. The home of the most powerful Black Dragon the combined worlds had ever known.

The island was once lush with vegetation and animal life. Until she decided to make her lair in the large mountain peak in the center of the island. The Dragon, knowing that the vegetation would shield anyone that may dare approach her Lair, went around the island and burned it all to the ground with her fiery breath. Once the dragon had completed her cleansing of the island she climbed the mountain and began digging to reach the mountain's core. There once she was finished and satisfied with the size and width of her Lair she began to transport all her treasure from her previous Lair.

As the pirates stared at the barren island they couldn't help but wonder how the Knight was ever able to reach the Dragon's Lair without being detected. Magic! It had to have been magic there was no there was no other explanation. The Knight must have had someone who could use magic help him get to the Great Wyrm in order to deliver the death blow, but who? A wizard, an elf, a vampire, who would be so bold to do this? Honestly it didn't matter whoever it was had opened the door for the pirates to gain the Dragons treasure they thought as they lowered the lifeboats and headed to shore. The trek across the island wasn't difficult because there was nothing but rocks and ash to walk over. The climb to the opening of the Lair was far more difficult however. The pirates had eight of their crew climb the sheer mount face carrying ropes to lower once they made it to the opening. This process took hours but eventually they were able to make it and lower the ropes for the other pirates to climb up.

The pirates could feel the energy of magic emanating from the Lair as they moved deeper into it, but they could sense the magic was definitely fading. There was a loud yell as the pirates entered the main cave and the corpse of the Dragon could be seen. The cave was filled with treasure and weapons of all kinds. The pirates were in a frenzy running all around the cave gathering anything they could for themselves. That's when the voice called to me, 'Free me!' I tried to ignore it at first thinking it was only my mind playing tricks on me. Then the voice became specific with what it needed to be done. 'I am The Heart of The Mother and I need you to remove me from her chest and bring me to her egg so my magic can free her son and keep the two worlds intertwined,' the voice said to me.

I don't remember doing it, but I took my sword and carved into the Dragons chest and removed the crystal. The other pirates saw the treasure I held in my bloody hands and demanded that I share it along with the other plunder they were gathering. The Heart had other plans and my men and I fought our way out of the cave and back to our ship. The other pirates despite the mounds of treasure were in hot pursuit of us and the treasure in my possession. We fought hard and long suffering many losses and I knew we couldn't get away at this rate. I enlisted the aid of my two closest officers and fled from the ship without the rest of the crew knowing. We did get away from the other pirates and made our way here with the intention of fulfilling the Hearts desire. We bought tools and made this hideout and I kept postponing bringing the Heart to the ocean in order to release the Dragon's heir. I just couldn't bear the thought of losing the crystal forever! I realized the Heart was contacting my officers and trying to get them to betray me, so I contacted the authorities and let them know where they would be. I watched them being dragged off in shackles and fled back here to our hideout. The Heart realized what I had done and that I had no intentions of ever fulfilling its request caused a great earthquake which caused the cave to collapse. That was not the only punishment the Heart had for me, it then set a curse upon me trapping me between the two worlds that I caused to be separated. I can never leave this cave and despite the Heart's numerous attempts at having someone free the Dragon's heir I will not allow it."

"No, no, no, this is why you never listen to the bad guy when they start telling you why they are doing the shit they do! Once they open their mouths we are supposed to run, that's what smart people do, their asses run! E.J. we need to go!" Sparrow screamed seemingly both annoyed and scared.

"Where's Tyree? And where the hell did the Heart go?" E.J. said, looking around the cave in disbelief. "Run!"

E.J. and Sparrow sprinted out of the cave and back into the tunnels leading towards the rope they had hanging in the other area. They heard a loud wail and the sound of something or somethings chasing after them. The corridor twisted and turned and the two ran without ever looking behind them to see what exactly was chasing them. They both had no desire to look because they were certain that the site would cause them to stop frozen where they were from fear.

"You stupid bastards! This was supposed to be a simple treasure hunt, nothing complicated! In, Out, Rich, that was what I was told. If I'd known you crazy bastards were chasing death I would have never agreed to come! You Know why? Because eventually you'll catch it or it'll catch you and the result from either outcome is what? Death!" Sparrow said, as he turned the corner and entered the room they had started in.

"Where's the rope? And Where's Tyree?" E.J. said, lifting his light to the ceiling and then shining it around the room.

"Is this the right room?" Sparrow asked, clearly terrified. "Are we in the right room?"

"This is the right room!" E.J. replied turning his light towards the corridor they had just exited and waiting to see what would burst from it and tear him and Sparrow apart.

Tyree pulled the rope up from the whole in the ground and stared in amazement as the whole closed. It took him a moment to gather himself, but once he did he realized he was standing in a pit. The whole they had made wasn't in a pit, he thought to himself, what the hell was going on.

"Give me your hand," a voice behind him said. "Hurry up, we don't have much time!"

Tyree turned around and allowed the hand being extended down into the pit to pull him up. He turned back and stared in disbelief. It was another Wolf Pit, just like the two that were only a few miles from here. This wasn't here before he thought!

"I....." Tyree was about to say something to the stranger when he made eye contact and everything went black.

"I'll take that." The tall, slender, brown haired stranger said, reaching into a pouch on Tyrees side and removing The Heart Of The Mother.

"Free Me!"

"Yes, yes, you're quite the impatient one aren't you. The stranger laughed. "Well come along."

The stranger motioned his hand and Tyree began walking along behind him.

"Freeing a Dragon and destroying this world as you know it is most likely going to be very draining and I'm going to need something to eat my young friend." The stranger said, holding the Heart before him as they walked towards the direction of the ocean.

LEGENDS

The scout knelt on the rocks and stared down into the valley. His party was still a few minutes behind him and from what he could tell their search for food was about to be fulfilled. He wasn't quite sure what kind of tree he was looking at, but it was beautiful. The smell coming from it was amazing and he could see some sort of plump fruits hanging from its branches. As he looked around it didn't appear to be any danger, so he slung his bow over his shoulder and headed down the rocks to the valley floor. He began sprinting in order to clear the open ground and get to the shelter of the tree. He was about halfway to the tree when he heard the loud buzzing sound and stopped to scan the area. He knelt down and felt the ground for vibrations, but there was nothing. Then as he shifted his eyes to the tree he gasped in amazement, the leaves were separating from the tree. He stood to his feet and stared as the leaves were now a large cloud above the tree. He knew there was no chance to run back to the rocks. All he could do was stare as the loud buzzing cloud rocketed towards him and once it got to him he screamed in agony!

The two elves cleared the trees and made it to a rock ledge that looked down into a valley. They looked out and could see what they believed to be their companion lying on the ground a few feet from a tree.

"Looks like Vani ate himself full and decided to camp," the taller of the two elves said, pointing his bow towards where his companion laid.

"He is dead Aruni and a fool," the smaller elf said, making a face in disgust.

"What, are you sure," Aruni replied, peering out to see if he could notice something the other elf saw and he didn't.

"The valley is shrouded in a glamour spell. That is a Feeding Tree," the elf said, moving to the edge of the rocks and speaking out a spell to lift the glamour. When he finished the valley seemed to morph and before them now was a pale, vile looking monstrosity of a tree with what looked like bloody tumors dripping gore and various dead animals and humanoids around it.

"The proper name is a hematophagia Tree," a tall slender man said, stepping from the shadow of a nearby tree. "And you must be Lani, my young elven friend!"

"Vampire!" The two companions yelled, drawing their weapons.

"Now is that nice? I didn't jump out and scream elves now did I," the slender figure said, folding his arms and leaning against a tree.

"Britannia, we are supposed to meet you at your castle. What's the meaning of this?" Lani asked, lowering his weapon, but not putting it away.

"Slight change of plans , I'm afraid. I would rather not have potential threats under my roof. I'm sure you must understand." Britannia said with a smile making sure to show his pointy fangs.

"What is that vile thing?" Aruni asked, pointing towards the tree.

"Oh excellent, please let me tell you. The Hematopagia trees are created by vampires to supply another form of sustenance in case we are unable to feed. They start out as normal seedlings, but instead of water we give them blood. A master vampire like myself will take lesser vampires and kill them by hoisting their bodies above the trees and letting their blood nourish it. After a while as the tree starts to grow instead of leaves the trees grow these symbiotic creatures that will kill creatures in a swarm style and bring the blood they drain from their victims back to the tree. The tree takes what it needs and then with the rest forms these blood fruits that we vampires find quite delicious.

The humans on Illunesti have a legend regarding such a tree. Their God made a majestic garden and in this garden he created man and woman. Here's where it gets juicy, the man was named Adam and the woman was named Lilith. Lilith drank the blood of animals, I guess she would be Mother to us vampires. Lilith turned some of the animals and brought them to the center of the garden. There she planted a seedling and fed it the blood of the creatures she changed. The tree grew big and strong and became known as The Tree Of The Knowledge Of Good and Evil. The human God saw what Lilith had done and cast her out of the garden, but not before she placed a glamour spell on it. The human God felt sorry for Adam and created another woman for him named Eve. Eve eventually ate from the tree and convinced Adam to do likewise. The tree's fruit is nourishment for a vampire, but if a mortal eats from it it enhances their awareness and makes them understand things better. The effect is temporary, but it was enough for them to question their God and get themselves kicked out of the garden he made for them. So you see these trees have been around for a long, long time." Britannia said, staring out at the tree lovingly.

"Well that's disgusting and vile, but you did mention the humans and Illunesti and that's why the Elven Council sent us. The rumors are that you have been able to travel to Illunesti all these centuries despite the Great Separation. The Council wishes to know if the news of Nalakara The Black Dragon being released from his egg by The Heart of The Mother is true and it the joining of our two worlds is upon us?" Aruni asked in a demanding tone.

There was a quick blur of motion and then a gurgling sound. Lani looked over at Aruni who was grasping at a gaping hole in his neck. Aruni collapsed to the ground dead and when Lani looked over at the vampire he was eating what could only be the chunk he removed from Aruni's neck.

"He was rude, little elf, shall we try this again?" Britannia said, licking the blood from his slender fingers.

"Fiend!" Lani screamed raising his sword at the vampire

"Oh little elf, I have no intentions of harming you. I need you to go back to the Council and inform them that their ancestral lands in Illunesti are about to be theirs again. The Dragon is freed, the joining of our worlds is upon us," the vampire said with a bloody smile.

"How can a baby Dragon do that which you say vampire," Lani asked.

"If he was a baby then no my friend he could not. However, he is not a baby dragon, the spell the mother placed on the egg allowed him to learn and see all the events going on around him. When the egg hatched he grew to full maturity and in doing so he called forth the other Dragons from this world to aid him in the joining." Britannia said, taking a cloth from his pocket and wiping the rest of the blood from his hands.

"Dragons have no more powers since the separation. What purpose would he have calling them to him, Lani asked, confused by the vampire's statement.

"The humans developed an energy source called New Cleared or something like that. Nalakara realized that if the dragons consumed this new form of energy it would rekindle the dormant magic in them. He brought them forth from this world and attacked and consumed all the weapons, machines, and energy sources that used this New Cleared power. The humans are is disarray, their leaders are panicking , and armies of Orcs and Goblins are streaming through world holes into Illunesti as we speak." Britannia said with a chuckle.

"What of the sword Xalundur is it not on Illunesti and was it not the weapon that killed the mighty mother Dragon and caused the worlds to separate. What is to prevent the wielder of the sword from killing Nalakara and preventing the joining. Why should we get our hopes up of reclaiming our ancestral lands just to have them dashed by one swing of a sword." Lani asked, staring at the vampire questioningly.

"Yes, Xalundur is actually in the possession of two brothers named Robert and Jaime Killingstroke. They are direct descendants of the knight who killed the Mother Dragon. That is how they got their last name, the knight came to be known as Todd Killingstroke after his victory. They are calling themselves the Brothers of Domaria, the knighthood their ancestor belonged to which faded out centuries ago. They are both good swordsmen, but neither would stand a chance against Nalakara. They have no sorcerer to aid them as did their ancestor, nor do they truly understand what it means to wield one of the Unblemished." Britannia said, patting the sword at his side.

"I hear stories of these weapons called the Unblemished. What are they and who is in possession of these weapons?" Lani asked with a curious look on his face.

"Fine! I did not realize that I would be giving history lessons to you when the Elven Council asked to send someone to meet with me. Centuries ago in the Dwarven mountain kingdom of Valladoon the dwarven miners dug deeper than they ever believed possible.

There in the deepest, darkest mine they found a vein of the purest ore they had ever seen. Despite checking it and rechecking it they found it to have no impurities, it was the stuff only dwarves could dream of. The king of Valladoon put his weapons smiths to work and from that rare ore they formed a war hammer and seven swords that they named the Unblemished. Once they were completed the weapons became sentient and could communicate with their owners. The weapons have passed through many a mighty warriors hands and even now are controlled by fierce and skilled fighters.

The war hammer is in the possession of the Sky King in his flying citadel. Xalundur is in Illunesti with the Brothers of Domaria. The Elven Ranger Hellian has one that he calls the Verdict. The Three Sisters of

Mercy each have one they hire out to whatever cause they deem just." Britannia was about to continue but was interrupted.

"Four Sisters of Mercy! You said Three. It's four. Tatiana, Kyra, Jayda, and Adriana." Lani said, realizing that he just rudely interrupted Britannia. "I apologize for being rude. I am truly sorry!"

"Yes, good catch, but do not do so again or I will send your head with a written explanation in your blood to the Council. Now where was I? Oh yes, well you were correct there were four sisters. However, during the Moonlight Wars between the Werewolves and Elves the Sisters and I found ourselves on opposite sides. The battles were bloody and fierce and on the final day of the war I found myself being followed by one of the Sisters as I made my escape. I did my best not to engage in one on one conflict with Kyra, but she was relentless. Finally she cornered me and I was left with no choice. Our blades clashed and sparked against each other as we thrust and parried each other's blows. Then her sword got through my defenses and bit deep into my side. Such pain I had never felt before, it drained me of my strength and I barely was able to dodge her killing stroke. She must not have thought me dodging the blow was possible because it caused her to lose her balance and stumble. In that one flawed second of her attack I struck and tore out her throat. She had the look of shock on her face, as if what had just happened to her was not possible. Oh, but it was! In my mind I heard the sword scream out with anguish at the loss of its wielder. I took the sword and the body of Kyra back to my castle with the sole purpose of making the sword mine. I drained Kyra of her blood and placed her blood into a tub and then I plunged the sword into it! I could hear the screams of the sword in my mind for days. The sword was being driven crazy and along with it so was I. One of us was going to break and luckily for me it was the sword. I had driven the sentient being inside the sword insane and turned one of the mighty Unblemished into the weapon you now see at my side. Let me introduce you to my pride and joy, the Tainted." Britannia said, drawing the sword from its sheath.

"You're mad! The Sisters are going to hunt you down and cut you to pieces for this desecration." Lani said, staring at Britannia in both shock and awe.

"You bore me now elf, It is time I took my leave of you! Go back and tell the Elven Council that the weapons from Illunesti will be arriving shortly. The Orcs and Goblins that are already attacking Illunesti have already been armed with these guns and weapons. The joining is upon us and there's nothing that anyone can do to stop it! Welcome to the Dawn of a New World little elf!" Britannia said as he seemed to fade into the darkness of the trees and vanish.

POEMS

POEMS

DARKNESS

Darkness

All around.

I cry out,

But there's no sound'

Is it night?

Or is it day?

There's nothing but Darkness

In my way'

Am I standing?

Or am I lying down?

I feel nothing

Where I should feel ground.

Darkness,

Darkness,

That only I can see.

For there's nothing but Darkness

Inside of me!

RED

While driving home in my Little Red Corvette

I found myself stuck at a Red light

I noticed the a beautiful Lady in Red

She was driving a Cherry Red convertible

She saw me and I turned Red in the Face

I realized my gas gauge was in the Red

So I pulled into a gas station next to the Red Roof Inn

I went in and bought some Red wine

With a Red Baron pizza for dinner later

And some Red Hots and Big Red gum

I hurried home to my Red nosed pitbull

Who jumped on my and almost committed Red Rum

I heard 99 Red balloons on the radio

Followed by Little Red Riding Hood

I decided to just watch the Red Sox game

Then top my night off with reruns of Redd Foxx

BLACK

While drinking my Black coffee

I remembered back to when I had long Black hair

And wore a Black leather jacket

I listened to Black Sabbath

At the club while drinking Black label

I would often come home with a Black eye

Or a variety of Black and blues

One night I got lucky at Black Jack

I invested my winnings in Black and Decker

And Black gold

Now I attend Black tie affairs

I wear Black tuxedos

And drive around in a Black limousine

I often eat at the Black Dog restaurant

Where they serve Black Angus steaks

And delicious Black Forest ham

Ending my day watching Black Adder

BLUE

First we ate a salad served with Bleu cheese dressing

Followed by a chicken cordon Bleu

For dessert we had hot Blueberry Pie

With Blue Bell ice cream on top

The song playing in the restaurant was Blue Velvet

After we strolled under a Blue Moon

On the shore near the ocean Blue

She had the most amazing baby Blues

I married her down in the Blue Bayou

GREEN

Watching the game on top of the Green Monster

While eating Green eggs and ham

With some fried Green tomatoes

We had a bet of Green backs on the game

Mike Greenwell hit the ball hard

It landed in the Green grass of center field

The Green light was given for the runner to score

My friend was Green with envy

I felt bad so i handed him a Wintergreen lifesaver

PINK

Pinky Tuscadero was watching the Pink Pantherv

But changed it to Pinky and the Brain

Enjoying a Pink Lemonade

And a eating a steak that was Pink in the middle

She decide to take out her Pink Cadillac

And drove to the Pink Flamingo lounge

She drank some Pink champagne on ice

People loved admired her Pink Chiffon

And her Pink Poodle skirt

She was truly Pretty in Pink

GOLD

I knew a girl with Golden hair

Who lived by the Golden rule

She grew up during the Golden age

And was a real Gold digger

She lived in the Golden state

Hoping to marry a Golden boy

Who would be her Golden goose

A real Gold mine

She'd spend her days listening to Golden oldies

Knowing her life was truly Golden

SILVER

I'm a star of the Silver Screen

But I wasn't born with a Silver Spoon

I was gifted with a Silver tongue

And i talked my way into the movie Silver Star

Then won an Oscar for my role in Silver Fish

Life does have a Silver lining

And I receive things now on a Silver platter

Many lives are just Silver plated

But not for this wise old Silver fox

WHITE

Dear Santa,

My baby sister would like a
White chocolate Santa and a DVD of Snow White.
My older sister would like tickets to see
Great White sharks and White whales.
My brother would like a trip to the White Mountains.
Where he can go White water rafting.
My mother would love a White gold ring with a
White pearl in the center.
My father would like the White Sox to win the World Series.
Then they can go and visit the White House as champions.
All I want is a fluffy White rabbit and to have a White Christmas.

Love,

Betty White

POMPEII

The Devil's blood is flowing from the mountain
Like the waters from a fountain
This once bright sunny day
Has turned into an ashen gray
People are fleeing down to the coast
No matter what happens:
I WILL NOT LEAVE MY POST!

Snow is falling from the sky
But this snow burns and hurts the eyes
The air is filled with an eerie sound
The baying of a thousand hounds
It's as if all of them have seen a ghost
No matter what happens:
I WILL NOT LEAVE MY POST!

The ground continues to tremble and shake
As people flee with whatever they can take
I hear people praying with all their might
And others wailing in terrified fright
The mountain unleashes it's invading host
No matter what happens:
I WILL NOT LEAVE MY POST!

People are being grabbed by the Devil's hand
And where they are is where they will forever stand
I hear screams of the dying all around
Any hope of salvation is nowhere to be found
I, myself in my armor begin to roast
No matter what happens:
I WILL NOT LEAVE MY POST!

THE ALAMO

Do to a battle fought many years gone bye
We will always remember a remorseful battle cry
It's the memory of one hundred and eighty men
Whose story has been written by many a pen
People know of the story wherever you go
And that's why we:
REMEMBER THE ALAMO!

It's in honor of the men whose lives were cut short
In that run down mission turned into a fort
Colonial Travis was in charge of it all
Bravely challenging the enemy to make the fort fall
His death was truly a devastating blow
And that's why we:
REMEMBER THE ALAMO!

Jim Bowie was known for fighting with a knife
He was a man who lived on the edge of life
An illness caused him to go to his bed
Where the enemy killed him dead
The story of his life and death continue to grow
And that's why we:
Remember THE ALAMO!

Davey Crockett came to Texas in hopes of land
Yet in this fort he would make his last stand
The shots he made with his rifle, "Betsy," were true
However, against overwhelming odds what could he do
His life has been immortalized in many a show
And that's why we:
REMEMBER THE ALAMO!

SALEM'S HALLOWEEN

Costumes being worn by young and old

People listening to ghost stories being told

Scary decorations hung everywhere

Ghostly sounds filling the night air

 Tourist visit all the haunted places

The Willows full of smiling faces

Eating salt-water taffy on the pier

It's Salem's busiest time of year

The Witch Museum line is long

Waiting people sing their favorite Halloween songs

The House of Seven Gables is a popular site

On this All Hallows night

Many are celebrating in the street

While happily greeting everyone they meet

You've never seen such jubilation

As the city of Salem's Halloween celebration

THE COSTUME

They said it would be fun just wait and see
Somehow I knew this fun was at the expense of me
One ran around getting articles of clothes
The other was doing god only knows
When the returned I could only stare
They had girls clothes and a curler for my hair
"What's this," I asked in shock
One said, "Stop acting like such a jock."
I'm just not understanding what you intend to do
They smiled and said, "Make a girl out of you!"
I got to my feet and was prepared to run
When one of them smiled and said, "It's all in good fun!"
So I sat while they applied makeup and curls
Turning this reluctant boy into a girl
When they finished they giggled with joy
Knowing the pain this was causing this boy
They placed a mirror in front of my face
And I could barely hold in my tears in place
I controlled myself without making a scene
For I had agreed to do this for Halloween
Sadly we still had to walk to the dance
Way too late to back out now, I had my chance
So as we walked side by side
I truly had no place to hide
People were laughing and beeping their car horns
Yes, I was the subject of many a scorn
At the dance the damn of laughter broke
As I was the subject of many a joke
I could only laugh to the lord above
Thinking to myself, the things we do for love
I'll remember that dance the rest of my life
For the girl who embarrassed me became my wife

BOSTON CHRISTMAS

It wasn't cold to me

I was to focused on all I could see

The Commons covered in snow

Little children watching a live Christmas show

Parents laughing with one another

A boy on a sled being pulled by his brother

Decorations hanging on every post

Cups of cocoa being raised in a toast

Carolers singing songs out loud

While people happily sing along from the crowd

Santa hats worn all around

Not one sad face to be found

A young couple heading out on a sleigh ride

As ice skaters pass with a graceful glide

Santa collecting money for the poor

Shoppers hurrying from store to store

A crowd watching artist turn ice into a swan

Couples buying Christmas decorations for their lawn

The spectators clapping as the lite the Christmas tree

Which is what everyone actually came to see

Yes, the city of Boston is a beautiful site

During the Christmas season at night

CHRISTMAS WISH

I dragged my tired body from bed
But couldn't lift my sleepy head
Normally i would wake with a bound
Yet this Christmas I barely made a sound
I was sure Santa had visited last night
Except inside I just didn't feel right
He probably brought all kinds of good stuff
That in all honesty should be enough
I just had my heart set on a certain thing
Which I doubted Santa would bring
I prayed to god with all my heart
And have been good from the very start
I even asked my mom and dad
But their reactions seemed rather sad
So as I walked from my room to the tree
I had a good glue to what I would see
Presents neatly set in different piles
With both my parents wearing big smiles
I found myself being knocked to the ground
By something making a yapping sound
It started licking my face
And jumping around from place to place
I felt myself beginning to cry
But the puppy licked the tears from my eyes
My parents were both laughing with joy
Knowing I wanted this more than any toy
So I held the puppy close to me real tight
Thanking god with all of my might

REVERE BEACH

Many different cars parked in a row

As other cars drive by real slow

Desperate to find a parking space

At this common meeting place

Girls in bikinis sitting on the sea wall

While guys drive by yelling out cat calls

People setting up lawn chairs to sit

With their radios playing the latest hits

Bikers peddling up and down the street

Yet most people prefer to just use their feet

It's easier to meet people that way

That's why people come here both night and day

This is the local gathering spot

Whether the season is cold or hot

Charlie's seafood is open all year round

Which has the best clams anywhere to be found

You can also enjoy the clear sky

Or talk to people as they're walking by

Some teens just love showing off their rides

Talking about their cars with pride

Older couples are out taking a casual walk

Eating ice cream as they talk

You can enjoy this under the moon or the sun

Because Revere beach offers something for everyone

BOSTON STRONG

There are many ways to cross a line
In a car, in a wheelchair, on your feet
Then there's ways that have no spine
That have nothing to do with the desire to compete

Hurting innocent people for no reason
Blowing up bombs in a public place
Committing a blatant act of treason
Killing innocent bystanders at a race

Then you hid like the cowards you are
Did you honestly believe you'd get away
As you can see you didn't get far
And for your crime you're going to pay

No one will ever keep us down for long
Our city stands the test of time
We are, "BOSTON STRONG"
And we proudly sing. "Sweet Caroline"

So as you face a sentence of death
Don't ask for mercy on our behalf
You're honestly wasting your breath
We hung our flags at half staff
You obviously didn't study history well
We're the city that started a revolution
Think on that as you rot in hell
For when Bostonians want justice there's only one solution

THE DANCE

She took my hand and danced with me
I could feel my heart beating frantically
Her smile made me catch my breath
That moment would of been the sweetest death
She never spoke a single word
If sher did I wouldn't of heard
I was lost in total rapture
My heart she did capture
My friends all watched in disbelief
For she was a jewel and I was a thief
I remember trying to speak
But the words came out soft and weak
That brought a smile to her face
Which brightened the entire place
I'd seen her in some classes before
But knew really nothing more
Never thought she'd give me the time of day
So now i didn't know what to say
I was in awe just to hold her
Heart racing with her hands on my shoulders
The song ended and we parted very slow
As if neither of us wanted to go
She gently kissed me on the cheek
My legs grew slack and weak
I wanted to thank her for the dance
But she never gave me the chance
She just smiled and walked away
Leaving my emotions in disarray
I'll ask her why she chose me to dance
And I'm sure I'll get my chance
We've been married now for thirty years
That's why I hold that memory so dear

SHE LOVES ME-SHE LOVES ME NOT

The first petal fell

I softly whispered her name

The second petal fell

I realized I was to blame

The third petal fell

I was a moth to her flame

The fourth petal fell

I became filled with shame

The fifth petal fell

I saw our picture in it's frame

The sixth petal fell

My wild heart became tame

The seventh petal fell

I was losing this game

The eight petal fell

My life will never be the same

SPIDER

Strands of sensitivity

Everywhere

Bodies wrapped in silk

A wasteland of the dead

It's dangerous to walk

Watch your step

Trust me

Don't get yourself caught

Vibrations bring death

The burglar alarm from hell

Wrong house to be trespassing

Make one false step

It'll be your last

Stuck

You're dead

Lunch bells ringing

And you're lunch

So

Bye, bye

Because she's coming

Here's a kiss for you

Embrace her darkness

Welcome to eternity

STAR

Do you know me

I've been popular since birth

I'm a household name

For what that's worth

People love me

My face is on every news stand

It's hard not being noticed

When you're in total demand

I'm a box office draw

On both stage and screen

Which isn't that great

Because everything i do is seen

I'm followed wherever I go

I'm never truly on my own

I understand that I'm famous

But everyone needs time alone

I love you

And I know you love me

But i need some space

Because it's making me crazy

TABLOIDS

I know a secret

I can't tell

Someone else will

Because gossip sells

Tell me something

It doesn't have to be true

As long as it's juicy

The magazines will pay you

Find out the latest rumors

Give me the dirt

I'll make sure it gets published

Who cares who it hurts

INTRUDER

It came through the window

Without making a sound

Crossed the room with ease

And touched all my belongings

But left no fingerprints

It caressed my face

Then kissed my uncovered arms

I awoke from this personal invasion

Scanned the room for this intruder

The curtains gently moved

I felt myself shudder

It was kissing me again

The breeze

WIDOWS WEEP

She stood upon the Widows Weep
Her thoughts constantly racing
Causing her to be unable to sleep
The breeze gently moves her gown
But she fails to even notice
Her face is locked in a frown
She sees many sails out on the sea
Yet none belong to her husband
Where on earth can he be
Rumors are all that reached her ear
Some bring her happiness
Others heighten her inner fear
She continues her vigil without fail
Constantly hoping
She'll see her husbands sail
Many nights waiting in the cold
Eyes focused on the horizon
Even when she's grown old

A FATHERS LOVE

I thought you entered the world so fast
Yet, in a blink
So much time has passed
You use to sleep on my chest
Like a tiny bird in a nest
When you were awake
The whole world was exciting and new
You fought so hard
To keep the day from being through
I had to laugh at your determination
As you rubbed your eyes
In frustration
You were learning and growing
Each passing day
At night I'd stand by your crib
And pray
You went from being so very small
To a curious speedster
In a crawl
Everything you saw you believed
To be a snack
You turned our living room
Into a race track
I would talk to you each night
You would babble with delight
I can't wait for us to really talk
Enjoying each others company
As we walk
Someday I'll share this
These moments we had
And just how much
I love being your dad

THE GIFT

To me you'll always be

The little girl on my knee

The angel so small

You use to have to crawl

You're god's special gift

That gave my heart a lift

Watching you learn to walk

Then discovering how to talk

Tucking you in at night

But leaving on the light

Singing you a lullaby

As you close your eyes

Someday you'll be all grown

Moving out on your own

I'm dedicating this rhyme

About our quality time

CINNAMON (1)

She came through the bedroom
In a fast run
Chased by our ferret
Cinnamon
Into the kitchen
The parlor
And back
With Cinnamon steadily
On the attack
He made a hissing sound
As he bounced
Trying to get close enough
To pounce
I had a big smile on my face
At this comical
Circular race
Round
And round they went
Til my daughter's energy
Was finally spent
She jumped onto the bed
In a single bound
And so did Cinnamon
With his hissing sound
I heard my daughter laughing
With glee
Because instead of her
Cinnamon was now
Attacking me

CINNAMON (2)

Under the couch
I saw Cinnamon scurry
As my daughter burst from her room
In a hurry
"He took my doll"
She cried
I couldn't hold back laughing
Even if I tried
"It's not funny"
She said in a serious face
I then remembered other items
Vanishing without a trace
I looked under the couch
But he was nowhere to be found
From inside the couch
I did hear a shuffling sound
I placed the couch on it's back
And discovered
Cinnamons secret shack
He looked at me in disbelief
As if though
We now were the true thieves
We retrieved the stolen doll
But that honestly was not all
Cinnamon had quite the stash
He had some more toys
Knickknacks
And even some cash

CINNAMON (3)

A little bundle of fur
Ran by me in a blur
I wondered where he was going
For he had no intentions of slowing
He tried to corner at top speed
Which he did not succeed
Hitting the wall didn't slow him down
He just made a hissing sound
Then into the bathroom he disappeared
Which was what i had feared
I heard the splash
Then a scream
A smile on my face
Started to beam
I looked through the bathroom door
Cinnamon was soaking wet
Staring at me from the bathroom floor
My daughter stared from her bath
You didn't have to do any math
"He started it"
Is what she said
I could only shake my head
I remember wanting a parrot
But her heart was set on a ferret

QUEEN JOSEPHINE AND MAXINE

Once upon a time there was a queen whose name was Josephine.
She was prettier than any woman who ever appeared on a movie
screen. Despite only being the age of eighteen.
She loved to be driven around in a nice limousine.
Then going to restaurants and eating the healthiest cuisine.
In fact this was her normal routine.
Now Queen Josephine had a younger sister named Maxine.
Who was only the age of thirteen.
The poor girl was the skinniest girl you have ever seen.
Due to the fact that she would only eat jelly beans.
Poor Queen Josephine didn't want to say anything that would
appear mean. Yet Maxine's diet was totally obscene.
So she decided it would be in Maxines best interest to intervene.
One day as they both sat relaxing in the mezzanine,
she offered Maxine a nectarine.
Maxine only wrinkled her nose, as if she was being offered a sar-
dine. Not to be discouraged, she decided to offer her a tangerine.
To her surprise at this Maxine seemed to be very keene.
Once Maxine took a bite her face seemed to take on a healthy
sheen, which was truly a beautiful sight to be seen.
Ever since that day Maxine has appeared on the cover of many a
magazine. As a shining example to everyone on the importance
of proper vitamins and proteins.

THE CAT AND THE CATERPILLAR

On a bright and sunny morning, a calico cat did a lazy stretch and morning yawning. Below the window upon which he lay, a little bug was making his bed, for a restful day.

Cat: My you're an ugly little thing

Caterpillar: That's because I have not yet taken to wing

Cat: What is that you say

Caterpillar: That I will not always look this way

Cat: No matter, you'll never be as beautiful as me

Caterpillar: Why don't you just wait and see

Cat watched as the little bug settled down for an afternoon nap.

He had to admit that he was now curious about this little chap'

Every morning Cat would check to see if the little bug had woken.

On one such morning Cat was surprised to find the little bed was now broken.

Cat: Where have you gone little one

Butterfly: To float on the wind for fun

Cat: Who's there?

Butterfly: Why it's me silly, up in the air

Cat: And just who are you supposed to be

Butterfly: The little bug, whose inner beauty is now free

Cat: You truly are a beautiful sight

Butterfly: I'm glad to see that you admit I was right

Cat: yes I was wrong to judge a book by it's cover

Butterfly: Or recognize the true potential of another

LEPERS WINDOW

Homeless and all alone

Listening to a preachers sermon

As I sit beneath the lepers window

Are people wearing their Sunday best

Does god love them more

And love me less

Will I always be on the other side looking in

When will my suffering stop

When will my blessings begin

I love the lord with all my heart

I read his word

My devotion did not just start

Are blessings being stored for a later day

Am I doing things right

Am I following the Lord's way

Once the people leave

Do they cherish the knowledge

Do they truly believe

These answers I truly desire

Because I long to go to heaven

And no desire to visit the fire

Being here is the right thing to do

For no matter where you sit

The Lord's love inside of you

FIRST LIGHT

As the sun shone down on me
Hot and bright
I remembered it was god who said
"Let there be light"
I marveled at his power
And his might
Because only god could say
"Let there be light"
And then there was light
I imagined how it would be
To have his sight
What he might have been thinking
When he saw the light
Then I looked around me
And I understood
Why it says in the bible
God saw the light
And it was good
He did realize something wasn't right
So he made an adjustment
And he divided the darkness
From the light
I look now at each day
In a different way
Because in the beginning
It was god who called the light, day
And in the darkness
When I'm filled with fright
I overcome my fear
Because it was god
Who called the darkness, night

PAUL

Once upon a time there was a man named Saul.

Who swore he'd wipe out the Christian belief once and for all.

That's until the lord Jesus decided to give him a call.

Jesus showed him how he was headed for a great fall.

That through him was the only way to reach God's heavenly hall.

Yet this wasn't a task that was small

Because you don't just walk in Christianity, you first have to crawl.

Saul decided he desperately wanted to become a believer after all.

He even changed his name from Saul to Paul.

In devoting himself to Jesus he did not stall.

From that day forth in Christian faith he stood tall.

He even spread the teachings of Jesus from Philippi to Gal.

BARTIMAEUS

As Jesus and his disciples left the city
A blind man sat on the roadside seeking pity
He heard the crowd calling Jesus name
And that it was from Nazareth that he came
This is the man who needed to hear his plea
So he shouter,
"JESUS SON OF DAVID HAVE MERCY ON ME!
The crowd rebuked him and told him to stop
But the sound of his voice did not drop
He could recognize things from touch and smell
Yet what they looked like he could not tell
He desperately wanted to see the colors of a tree
So he shouted,
"JESUS SON OF DAVID HAVE MERCY ON ME!
He heard the crowd tell him to draw near
He tossed his cloak and approached without fear
Jesus asked, "What do you want me to do for you"
This question was truly too good to be true
Jesus could give him the ability to see
So he shouted,
"JESUS SON OF DAVID HAVE MERCY ON ME!

SINNER'S PLEA

Pages turn each passing day

Time, like life, is passing away

We cannot dwell on yesterday

When we are only promised today

Tomorrow isn't guaranteed

The pale horseman may come on his steed

Our lives are always on the brink

Death is a well from which we all drink

Many are afraid of how it might taste

Some want it served to them without haste

Does your hand on the doorknob of eternity shake

Or is your entering it a decision to make

Can you say it was a righteous life you led

Will you be one of the living when your bodies dead

These thoughts race through my mind

Because I was once spiritually blind

So if I'm only promised here and now

I'm going to do the best I know how

Lord Jesus please hear this sinner's plea

Let your Holy Spirit shine bright inside of me

THE DENIAL

Jesus was led away without resistance
While Peter watched and followed at a distance
To the house of the high priest they went
For it was from him the soldiers were sent
Peter was sitting in the courtyard by the fire
He knew that the situation Jesus was in was dire
A servant girl was slowly walking by
But when she saw Peter she stopped and cried
"You also were with Jesus of Galilee"
Peter realized it would do him no good to flee
So he denied her accusation with a shout
"I don't know what you're talking about"
He rose from the fire and walked away
Then he went out to stand by the gateway
Another servant girl was making sure everyone was fed
She saw Peter standing there and said
"This fellow was with Jesus of Nazareth"
Peter was certain the wrong answer would be his death
So he denied Jesus saying as fast as he can
"I don't know the man"
A man in the crowd looked over at Peter and attested
"You're the one who was in the garden when he was arrested"
Peter answered him without a thought
"I am not"
Immediately a rooster crowed
Then it was as if time just slowed
Peter remembered the words Jesus had spoken
Words he felt could easily be broken
"Before the rooster crows, you will disown me three times"
Jesus had correctly predicted Peters crime
He denied the Lord who he swore he loved passionately
And because of this he went outside and wept bitterly

GETHSEMANE

Jesus went with his disciples to a place called Gethsemane

A garden across the Kidron Valley

from where he and his disciples came

He said to them, "Sit here while I pray"

As he sadly walked away

He took Peter and the two sons of Zebedee, James and John along

He was hoping for him they could be strong

He began to be sorrowful and troubled

It seemed as if sins of the world had suddenly doubled

Then he said, "My soul is overwhelmed to the point of death

And it appeared to pain him even to take a breath

Yet he somehow continued his plea

Saying, "Stay here and watch with me"

Going a little farther, he fell on his face

Overcome by the sins of the whole human race

Even though his sacrifice was already fated

He dreaded the thought that he and his father were to be separated

An angel from heaven appeared and strengthened him

For the heavenly host knew that separation

from God was truly grim

His sweat was like drops of blood falling to the ground

And from his body came a sobbing sound

On his face he humbly stayed

With anguish he earnestly prayed

The heavens and earth stood still

When he said, "Yet not as I will, but as you will

He arose exhausted from his weeping

The he returned to his disciples and found them sleeping

He asked peter, " Couldn't you men keep watch for one hour

Yet he knew their sleep was induced by Satan's power

So he tried to stress how important this was as he began to speak

"The spirit is willing, but the flesh is weak

He hoped they could do this for him as he walked away

Once again falling on his face to pray

For a second time the heavens and earth stood still

"Yet not as I will, but as you will'

It was truly hard for him to believe

To be separated from the one whose love never leaves

His disciples were sleeping again upon his return

They still had so much to learn

To die for them is why he came

And they would greatly suffer in his name

So he left them to pray once more

Praying exactly what he had prayed before

For the third time the heavens and earth stood still

"Yet not as I will, but as you will"

IT IS FINISHED

Darkness came over the whole land at about noon
The life of Jesus would be ending soon
They laughed and joked at his torment
Casting lots for his garments
The predictions of the prophets were coming true
"Father forgive them for they know not what they do"
One also crucified joined in his scorn and ridicule
The other called his friend a fool
He knew his chances to enter heaven were slim
He asked when Jesus entered his kingdom to remember him
Jesus didn't even think twice
He said, "Today you will be with me in paradise"
Jesus noticed his mother sadly weeping
He decided to make sure she would be in safe keeping
Jesus said to her, "Woman here is your son'
As he looked from her to his best loved one
To him he said, "Son, there is your mother'
He watched as they cried and hugged one another
Then he cried out at the hour of three
"My God, My God, Why have you forsaken me"
Jesus looked around and said, ":I am thirsty"
A soldier thought this a request for mercy
Into some wine vinegar he gave a sponge some dips
Then lifted the sponge to Jesus lips
Jesus said loudly so all could hear it
"Father, into your hands I commit my spirit
His bodies strength was totally diminished
He gave up his life saying, "It is finished"

MARY (1)

I can't believe the things I've done

The sins

My body shakes as I sob

I couldn't speak if I tried

My tears are soaking his feet

They are still dirty from his journeys

I will use my hair to dab away the dirt

Where I clean

I will kiss

I'm not worthy

My eyes cannot look upon him

I only pray

He'll grant me

Forgiveness

MARY (2)

I take in every word

Sitting at his feet absorbing wisdom

My sister doesn't understand

He doesn't care how the house looks

He doesn't want a drink

Or something to eat

He's here to give

To feed us

To give us the way to his father

And I intend to listen

And learn

As should she

As should

Everyone

FENCES

The sun still warms the body
Yet inside I'm cold and lonely
The grass is greener on the other side
I can see it
But it's untouchable
Picnic tables aren't so inviting
Viewing them through razor wire fences
Lifes truly no picnic
I never really noticed
How beautiful nature is
Until taken from me
Everything from outside
Now only visions in my mind
Like a masterpiece of art
Unable to step to it
Protected by a guardrail
My mind full of pictures
A butterfly in the wind
Tree limbs swaying in the breeze
Horses roaming a field
Breathtaking
And yet also heart breaking
Why are zoo animals so sad
Become one
View the world through a fence
It's only right there
Inches
Within my reach
Yet untouchable
Don't feed the animals
What don't they want us to consume
Hope

THE LIGHT

As sure as the sun is the light of the sky

The light of the body is the eye

The sun may warm our outer skin

What we see with our eyes warms within

If they fill our body full of light

Then the Holy Spirit inside us shines bright

And let us put on the armor of light

So we can face the enemy in our spiritual fight

Jesus said, "I am the light of the world

Thereby his true nature was unfurled

No followers of him walk in darkness

For they have the light of life

Cutting thru darkness like a knife

Walk as children of the light

Growing and empowered by his might

BROKEN

You only hurt
The ones you love
Jesus, I love you
I must
Ten Commandments
Broken
Well not all ten
Myself
Myself
Okay all ten
Why did you die
For me
Who asked you too
I'm not worthy
Temples are wholly
My body is one
Defiled
Look up sins
I've done them
I may created them
Sorry
I want to be good
Can i start over
Is there a rewind
Freeze frame
Something
Yup, I'm stuck
Can we walk
Will you carry me
I really need it
Religion
I have tried
See my mess
And still you love

SHEEP

I am lost
You can look
You won't find
Over the mountains
Through the woods
Valleys
Hills
It's hopeless
I know where i am
But won't tell
I'm not ready
Maybe someday
Just not yet
Your cries are heard
Your love is appreciated
I know you care
At least someone does
I'll reach the point
Of no return
Then will you seek
Will you find
I will beg
Plead
Repent
Weep
Please listen
You're all i have
Be my shepherd
Lead me back home
Dear Lord

TRUTH

Hypocrite look at me
Don't answer the mirror
LOOK AT YOURSELF
Why are you so angry
LOOK AT YOURSELF
Where did you go
Wash away the guilt
Scrub hard
You changed
Lost, lost forever
Are you happy
Please everyone
But your lost
You forgot your own happiness
Who's watching
Who really cares
The show will go on
Because you're a clown
Painted for them
Wet pillows
Tearful dreams
The price of popularity
Hidden insecurities
I won't tell
Because you won't listen
The person you were
Now dead
If you're not you
Then who
Change isn't always good
Bury the past
When you were real
FAKE

DAMN

Not there
But guilty
Not there
But innocent
Do i feel shame
Actions are sentences
Words are condemning
The blood is the cure
How long was I sick
Evil
Good
Misunderstood
The mirror shows truths
The face is a story
Lines tell all
Heartache
Sorrow
Pain
Who's to blame
Answers at bottle bottoms
Responsibility pushed away
Excuses embraced
Where was I
In life
Books hold answers
Depending on the writer
The Book of Life
The Book of the Lamb
The Book of Death
What did I write
My finish

DESTINY

I took a right

Was the left correct

Did i miss destiny

Is it fate

What's the grand scheme

Who's directing me

I made the decision

Or did I

Preplanned

Possibly

God only knows

I can't worry

Whatever happens

Happens

Outcomes the same

Death

Can't avoid it

Whatever path I take

So let's ride

GRADES

I'm being tested
I need a number two pencil
I just can't answer
I never could
I love erasers
They make things go away
Pens hard to erase
It smudges
I should know
I tried
What's the question
Life
Lived it
Not impressed
Move along
Times being wasted
That's life
Give
Or take
Give
It's not worth it
Ask someone
Is that considered cheating
Who's in charge
Parents
Teachers
Bosses
God
Correct my answers
I'm a pen
Can't you tell
What's my grade
Incomplete

FALSEHOOD

I need a partner
Cards
Tennis
Love
Life
Glue sticks
Relationships don't
What's my shoe size
Does it fit good
Shug
We didn't
I've outgrown my shirt
And you
Isn't that how it goes
It's not you
No it is
I lied
It hurts
But it's for the best
Your best
My worst
The thrill is gone
When did it start
It's our anniversary
Of the end
Do we celebrate
Do we remember
I love you
Empty
No emotion
Til death do us part
I'm still alive
Have a heart
Mine

SENTENCED

Light shining
Through a screen
Ants rule my room
I share my food
The night's are cold
So's the concrete
My bed is hard
Metal usually is
Voices through my door
It's locked
Always
I have a sink
Which is also my toilet
They're connected
As am I
I read my bible
It reads me
One conclusion
I failed
Was i winning
Do winners have barbwire
Maybe they do
We all have hearts
Closed
Encased
No one enters
The pain can't leave
Pick your prison
We're never truly free
We have ourselves
I'm sick
Society says so
God hasn't yet
But he will

RUN

I just can't run anymore

I'm tired

Exhausted

My life is in havoc

I can hear them

Dogs of War

They've been released

Searching for me

I see the light

It's on me

Found

Runs over

I surrender

Praise God

Lead me home Lord

TRY

Bells ringing

Whistling sounds

Skeeball

Only a few tokens

Hit the hundred hole

Rack up the points

Don't gutter ball

Try to aim straight

It's hard being small

Use two hands

Need the tickets

To get something good

That's what matters

Have a blast

You can do it

Have to try

If you fail

Try again

GAMES

I hear love is just a game

I just don't think it's the same

Can you compare a relationship

To a game of Battleship

It's harder to be man and wife

Then playing the game of Life

You deal with way more stress

Compared to a game of Chess

Teaching your children to understand

Life is harder than a game of Candyland

It can be way more sadder

Than Shoots and Ladders

That meeting your future spouse

Isn't like winning with a full house

Love is many things, that's true

But can't be solved like Clue

THANK YOU

Mom

I cause you misery

Despite sacrifices you made

For our family

Your the one who taught me

How to be strong

Without your guidance

I would of turned out wrong

You did everything for us

Barely making a fuss

Lifting us when we were down

Making us smile instead of frown

Gold truly broke the mold

You're worth way more than

Money

Diamonds

Gold

Made in United States
North Haven, CT
01 January 2023

30482808R00125